FRASER VALLEY REGIONAL LIBRARY

D0546929

ADVICE FOR TAXIDERMISTS & AMATEUR BEEKEEPERS

ADVICE FOR TAXIDERMISTS & AMATEUR BEEKEEPERS

A NOVEL BY
ERIN EMILY ANN VANCE

Stonehouse Publishing
www.stonehousepublishing.ca
Alberta, Canada

Copyright © 2019 by Erin Emily Ann Vance
All rights reserved. No part of this publication may be
used without prior written consent of the publisher.

Stonehouse Publishing Inc. is an independent
publishing house, incorporated in 2014.

Cover design and layout by Anne Brown.
Printed in Canada

Stonehouse Publishing would like to thank and acknowledge
the support of the Alberta Government funding for the arts,
through the Alberta Media Fund.

Albertan
Government

National Library of Canada Cataloguing in Publication Data
Erin Emily Ann Vance
Advice for Taxidermists and Amateur Beekeepers
Novel
ISBN 978-1-988754-18-5

PROLOGUE

Agatha pinned dead bees into tiny frames, while her sister, Sylvia, watched her infant daughter throw blocks at a cat with disinterest. They unknowingly did these things while their sister burned to death and their brother pulled tiny organs out of a rat with the care of a surgeon performing a heart transplant.

In elementary school, Margot Morris made a volcano for the science fair. It wasn't until she had school children of her own that she felt the heat that she imagined that day in the gymnasium, watching the baking soda and vinegar bubble over her brother's lego figures.

When Sylvia Black was fourteen, she went away to summer camp and kissed a boy for the first time. She remembers almost nothing except that it was night time, they were in an outhouse, and she could smell his breath almost as well as she could smell the shit and piss wafting from the hole in the ground. She was repulsed but found herself pulling him into her by his bowl cut. She felt the thrill of control in being just a little bit stronger than the boy.

When Agatha Morris was pregnant with her first baby, it was January. The snow was densely packed, brown and icy. She slept with all of the windows open, naked. Her husband slept in a thermal sleeping bag he'd borrowed from Sylvia. One morning, Agatha woke up and she remembered how it felt to be cold and she knew the baby was gone.

Teddy Morris once used an entire bottle of his sister's foundation to coat his body in a cool peach glow. He wore a black wig he stole from his school's theatre department. He stared in the mirror in his parents' bedroom, seeing for the first time how his body was shaped by the same genetic hands of his sisters and mother. He felt like a solid, human form and not like a ghost. Except for his eyes. They remained a milky red, standing out against pigmented skin even more violently than they did against his translucent body.

CHAPTER 1

The front window of Wayward Coffee Company is dusty. Three years ago, the owner commissioned a high school kid to paint a cartoon Christmas mural on it. No one ever bothered to wash it off. From a dusty yellow armchair a five-foot fish statue is visible out the window by a saskatoon berry bush that reaches towards the street. There is not a lot of fishing around here, just the Sheep River. It's not like the Valley lies close to a lake or the coast.

In front of the dusty Christmas window, beside the dusty yellow armchair and on a dusty side table, lies a newspaper under a ceramic mug full of old coffee, a constellation of blue mold drifting from one side of the mug to the other, dragging along with it a yellow membrane of milk and honey. The newspaper is missing the sports section, and is open to the classifieds, an obituary circled in pencil.

Margot Morris 1990-2015
Lola Morris 2007-2015
Luna Morris 2010-2015

Known by her friends and family as an incredible mother, loving sister, and devoted friend, Margot Morris will be deeply missed by the community.

Margot and her daughters, Lola and Luna, passed away unexpectedly on July 21st. They are survived by Margot's older siblings and their families; Sylvia

(Matthew) Black and her daughter Ella, Edward "Teddy" Morris, and Agatha Morris (Nicholas Bloom).

Margot, Lola, and Luna were predeceased by Margot's parents (Lola and Luna's grandparents), Casper and Lulu, as well as Margot's great aunt (Lulu and Lola's great-great aunt), Theodosia Morris, and their border collie, Lucy, who passed away in May.

Margot was born and raised in The Valley, and has worked as manager of the Wayward Coffee Co. since 2005. Customers remember her smiling face and her excellent lattes. There is a memorial wall set up at the coffee shop where members of the community are encouraged to post photos and messages to Margot and her family in this difficult time.

A celebration of life will be held on July 26th at the Moth and Cradle funeral home. In lieu of flowers, Margot, Luna, and Lola's family ask that donations be made to the local SPCA."

The Valley is quiet. The coffee shop closed. Across the street is an old home with peeling paint squeezed in between the senior's centre and a commercial woodshop. A screen door bangs into the concrete step, slightly off its hinges in the wind. A dog with chewed up ears barks, tied to a post with an old piece of climbing rope. The Valley is the sort of town where the quieter inhabitants are named by a single feature. The one-armed man lives across from the café, where most days, Crossword Wanda can see him let his cat out from her seat by the window.

Turning blue in a dollar store frame, a 1998 article in Avenue Magazine (Calgary Edition), describes The Valley as a "callback to the midcentury, where women don't leave the house without being made-up, and the men still have dirt on their boots." A solitary bee buzzes against the window, avoiding a spider web in the corner, a slight thunk

thunk

thunking as it runs out of breath.

"In the Valley, visitors will find a 57 chevy, powder blue, parked-outside of the kitschy 50s-themed diner, 'Chips.' They can get a chocolate malt and then carry on next door to 'Pop's' barbershop, before heading out of town to witness a church sermon lead by an Elvis impersonator."

The bee, frantic, breathes in too much dust, and dies. Over the next hour, the spider drags it to the web, and wraps it in silk.

CHAPTER 2

Three days earlier, Margot Morris and her daughters' bodies have yet to be discovered. In the early hours of that Saturday morning, Agatha Morris thinks about the ethics of beekeeping. She's never been one to smash a spider under her shoe heel, but here she keeps thousands of creatures as her own. She kills them when she sees fit, steals their honey. She has a birthmark on the underside of her elbow that she stares at while contemplating these questions. Her almost-ex-husband once likened it to the size and colour of a tomato hornworm or a five-spotted hawk-moth.

When she catches the purple blotch in the mirror she thinks of the stillbirths. They are each garden snails; that one marvel that she wants to save and keep in a terrarium on her night stand or kill and gut and glue on a backing to pin to her jacket.

In the garden, Agatha thinks of the delicious struggle of damaged hens with their feathers plucked out. She thinks of the threat of slow bees, and the way that the books tell her how to keep these things, but not how to keep herself.

Agatha's grandmother raised chickens. Mostly for eggs. Once for meat. The meat birds grew from honey chicks to giant, prehistoric monsters. Agatha's brother, Teddy, liked to pluck out their feathers and run, delighted at the dinosaur-like chase. "I'm in Jurassic park!" he would yell until their grandmother scolded him in a thick Welsh accent.

Bees, Agatha thought, were unlike livestock in that they were always beautiful, even in death and frenzy. One summer, when a group of workers balled a queen in Agatha's hand, she looked on with delight and fascination.

She contemplates this while she dons her armour: a fencing mask salvaged from the dumpster of Oilfields High, a hazmat suit scavenged after the floods in High River, a pair of ski boots from Goodwill, and a pair of gardening gloves topped with dish gloves. Her glasses bump against the inside of the mask. She trudges through the uncut grass, chewing the skin of her bottom lip, coaxing a loose strand of skin into her mouth. It's like chewing on a piece of turkey leftover in your teeth after lunch, she thinks.

The telephone rings back in the house, and Agatha chews harder, grabbing onto another bit of skin with her teeth. It's probably one of her sisters, checking up on her as usual. *Has the divorce gone through? How are you coping? Are you sure about this, Aggie? He's a good man, one of the only ones left. Maybe you can try in vitro again. What about adoption? One of the mums at the school fosters, you could look into that, maybe.* Maybe even her brother. *Come over when the divorce is final and me and Tas will help you celebrate properly. I've got a bottle of Crown left over from Christmas.* One of her nieces, maybe, calling to tell her about a new craft they made at summer camp. *Look, Aunt Aggie! It's a bee, a bee made of beeswax, for you!*

As Agatha gets closer to the hives, the ringing fades and the buzzing becomes audible. She breathes slower now, smells the lavender. She lets the activity of the bees burrow into her ears until she thinks *yes, I am the hive. The hive may have a queen bee, but I am the keeper of that queen.* The puffed purple columns sit to her right, lining the path that Matthew promised he'd mow last Tuesday but now it's Monday and what the hell happened to that? No one is in the garden yet, thank god. Trailing a hand along the lavender, Agatha gazes at the large plot. The sunflowers that nobody planted but that thrive more than any other living thing in the garden stare down at the broad beans. The small gazebo with the tea table stands proud, facing the wildflowers and the trees.

Sometimes the other gardeners get to Agatha's before she wakes up. This pisses her off. After she separated from her husband, Agatha started the community garden on the advice of her sisters, for companionship, though she prefers to work alone. Today the sun runs its fingernails down her back. It is silent, except for the phone, which is ringing again. Except for the buzzing, too. But Agatha thinks this to be a vibrant silence, a living silence. She ignores the phone. Probably one of her sisters or her brother-in-law. It's not her almost-ex-husband. It's probably her sisters, or her brother-in-law. Maybe her nieces. Definitely not her ex-husband.

Agatha peers inside the hives, looking at the thick, white honey. Pearlized, caramelized, shiny like milk diamonds or stiff silk. She pulls on her lips with her teeth, catching on the scar beneath her bottom lip. What would it be to swallow a hive whole? To swallow herself whole?

Today, Agatha must re-queen one of the hives. She only gets to this maybe once or twice a year, and she smiles, knowing that nobody is here to interrupt her. She doesn't have time to answer the phone. No time for small talk or gossip or to humour Sylvia when she puts the phone to her infant daughter's lips. When it's time to assassinate the queen and send in a replacement, nothing else matters. Each queen that Agatha must kill is placed into a killing jar filled with tissue paper and nail polish remover and carried back to the house. After the breath escapes the insect, Agatha pins her and places her in a small wooden frame. Agatha sleeps with fourteen dead queens above her head.

This queen was too slow in the womb. Agatha looks at the meagre harvest and sighs. Most beekeepers dispatch the queen, but if Agatha were a bee, she'd rather be immortalized than left to find another home. Besides, she can't risk what might happen if the disgraced queen were to return. The queen is right where Agatha suspects her to be, surrounded by workers who try again and again to speed her slow womb, and Agatha thinks that she herself is not unlike the queen. In a swift motion, she scoops the queen into the jar. The queen buries herself in the shredded tissue and shivers. Agatha watches as the queen dies a reasonably quick death from the fumes. The queen flickers, the life leaving her. Agatha holds the jar up to her eye as the bee gives one final twitch, like the last involuntary movement before sleep. Agatha checks on each hive before taking the queen inside.

***

At 11 a.m. on Saturday, Margot Morris' neighbour reports a small fire. He hadn't seen or smelled anything the night before, but a corner of Margot's house has blackened and collapsed inward. Catacombs of ash jut out of the small house, beige with teal trim. It has the look of an abandoned wasp's nest. The firefighters are at the house by 11:10, and by 11:15 they are shaking their heads at the old man, who smells of plastic-bottle rum. None of Margot's other neighbours noticed anything the night before. An arson expert is called in from Calgary and she is baffled.

Outside of town, Sylvia Morris fills the cab of her truck with smoke, ashing her cigarette into an old Slurpee cup, the orange syrup at the bottom of the cup congealing around butts and ashes. She sings along to the radio under her breath and stares over the dash of the pick-up. Her daughter coos. Sylvia coughs out the words to a Savage Garden song, her voice low and warbling. She drives with Ella towards the mountains. The radio drifts into static and out again as they curl around the hills and valleys. Accompanying Sylvia's singing is a soft mewing from the backseat. Duct-tape holds the rear-view mirror to the roof. She sees her daughter watching the road out of the corner of her eye. A bee sits on Ella's wrist, calm. Sylvia wants to swat it away, but she doesn't want the insect to sting the infant. She knows Ella isn't allergic to bees, but doesn't want to deal with the crying.

"We can't afford to feed any more mouths. Your papa's working so hard as it is." The child grins at the bumblebee and drools. Of course, she doesn't understand, she's just an infant. She hasn't even seen the kittens, their eyes still glued shut from birth.

Sylvia sucks on her cheeks until they fill the space between her teeth and spill into the back of her jaw where her wisdom teeth were pulled from. Her adult braces rub against them. She cracks her neck loud, and rolls down the window. She butts out the dying cigarette in the slurpee cup and spits out the window.

"The coyotes are fast and hungry. They won't suffer." Sylvia cracks her knuckles against the steering wheel, digging her joints into the sun-worn rubber. "Your granddad woulda just killed them, stuck a needle in them. Made them into toys."

They curve around the side of a hill and the radio dissolves into static one last time. Sylvia slams on the breaks. A little girl in a red dress is standing in the road.

"Jesus Christ!" The little girl looks exactly like her youngest sister did as a child and for a moment she thinks it must be one of Margot's daughters. Ella begins to scream in her car seat.

"Shh... Baby it's okay! Mommy has to leave the car for a second but I'll be right..." Sylvia undoes her seatbelt and reaches for the door handle but the girl is gone. Shaken, Sylvia sits back in the seat. The kittens are crying and so is Ella. Sylvia's hands shake as she puts the vehicle in drive. The radio screeches.

"SHUT UP! Everything, just quiet!" Ella stares at her mother and cries louder.   Sylvia reaches into her pocket, feeling for her cell phone, but she must have forgotten it at home.

CHAPTER 3

When the coroner separated the skin from the bone, maggots had spread so heavily that it looked like they had replaced the woman's veins and arteries. *What a fertile body,* she thought, marveling at the colonization of flesh. Not unusual for bodies left for a few days. But one night? She loved to see this decomposition, and was lucky in that she barely had a sense of smell anymore. Only when she slid the body back into the metal locker did she notice something queer. Queerer than a triple death-by-freak-accident. Back in the dark recesses of the locker, the blood casings began to glow. Discarded cocoons coated with glow-in-the-dark ink sat idle inside the body of Margot Morris. She pulled the body out again quickly, the breasts bouncing, flayed open from her chest cavity. In thinner corpses, the breasts usually get trapped in the armpits, but Margot Morris has enough flesh to prop them up. They were white on white, like pull-apart buns not yet cooked to golden-brown. She then pulled out the three other bodies: the eight-year old, the five year old, and the fetus, roughly five months She slowly pushed them into the lockers, eyes glued to the back of the boxes, her face close to the toes of the dead women. She squinted, searching for the glow. It was late, she had probably just imagined it. It was nothing, she was certain. She turned to wipe her nose.

"Shit," she muttered, feeling a clot slide down her right nasal cavity, feeling the heaviness in the space between her nose and throat. A small drop of blood was on her sleeve. As the coroner turned to grab a paper towel, she again saw the glowing. A glob of blood fell to the floor as she breathed heavily, watching the glow from the corner of her eye, afraid to turn one way or the other lest she see it fully or it disappear. The nosebleeds were becoming more and more frequent, and she was hoping that she could stave another one off until 2 p.m. tomorrow, when a scientific journalist was slated to interview her about The Valley's first coffin birth.

The coroner looked at the clock. 9 p.m.. Time to clean up. She sighed, and readied a cigarette, a chunk of paper towel shoved into her nostril. In the dim light outside the morgue, the coroner looked up at the moon, yellow and round as a bumblebee's bottom.

***

Some bees come from packages. Some are kept over the winter. Agatha follows the same protocol for both. She inspects the bee colonies to ensure that the queens are there and laying eggs. She must ensure that there is no sign of disease and that the colony has enough stores to last until the first nectar. When the bees cover seven of the frames in the top super then Agatha adds another super. The extra supers are in the basement, where Agatha keeps the books from before.

Single-bloom flowers in yellow, blue, and purple are the best for attracting bees. Agatha tends to her garden of echinacea, salvia, verbena, lavender, mallow, primrose, and hollyhock. She collects and presses the flowers, sometimes preserving them in resin or affixing them to dioramas with insects or birds. The family taxidermy business is booming, and helping Teddy out with it keeps Agatha busy, so busy that sometimes it is as though 'before' never existed. She can almost forget all of the dead babies and estranged lovers when she is in the garden, with her bees, or while she is pinning insects and pressing flowers. She can pretend that "before" was not a wasteland of miscarriages and stillbirths and divorces and tears and pain. Almost.

Not every day is a killing day, so Agatha leaves the killing jar inside her office until the next queen must die. She holds tender the specimens in her office and makes nectar for the hummingbirds.

"1 cup sugar.

4 cups water.

Bring to a boil.

Let cool."

***

Transporting bodies is a tricky business. The dying keep no regular hours, and the undertaker has not known uninterrupted sleep in twenty-two years. The Valley keeps him busy, especially since his business is small. He had a handful of employees and interns in the early 2000s, when *Six Feet Under* popularized the industry, but most college-aged kids who watched HBO and made dark collages while listening to sad songs weren't actually cut out for funeral directing. Sure, the media tried to show the gritty reality of death, but this was still television, and even "R" ratings didn't account for the times an undertaker knocked a dead baby off of the counter into a mop bucket, or the times the undertaker blew his nose into a handkerchief while driving only to realize that the same handkerchief had been used hours earlier to fill a leaking cavity.

The volatile Alberta weather makes life difficult for funeral directors. He once slipped on the ice with a cardboard boxes containing the remains of newborn twins. Body boxes come in different sizes, custom made for infants like cases made to house fragile rare books. The preemies and miscarriages were in tiny boxes, the full-term stillbirths slightly larger. Normally, he had a small cart, but that day the cart was missing, and he estimated that the tread on his sneakers could carry him to the van. Agatha Morris' milk-purple, stillborn twins skidded across the black ice, their wrinkled bodies still curled into each other like stale lima beans. The placenta shot out underneath his van. As he cradled the frozen babies in his arms, he breathed deep. A nurse walked around the corner in a wool sweater with a cigarette in her hand. She glared at him as she blew smoke in his direction, a look of disgust spreading up her face as she sucked on the cigarette before throwing it into the street and running inside.

Summers weren't much better. The hot sun would cook bodies if he didn't get to them quickly enough, and each year a different insect seemed to swarm. Flies, one year, caking the window ledges of the funeral home. Grasshoppers, another. Their chirping kept him awake with visions of burnt limbs and severed appendages dancing in his head.

It is, as he calls it, the year of the wasp when Margot Morris is murdered. Every house in the valley has decoy wasps nests that look like Japanese paper lanterns hanging from their porch lights. He has two deaths from allergic reactions by July—it wasn't easy to get a face swollen to twice its size ready for an open casket. When he receives the call from the RCMP about 3 bodies needing to be picked up after autopsies, he says a quick prayer that swollen-shut eyes aren't part of the deal.

***

Teddy Morris leans against the bar at the coffee shop, inhaling coffee beans and staring at himself in the shiny metal surface of the large espresso machine. *It looks like an airstream*, he thinks, as the barista hands him his Americano. Teddy Morris empties eight packets of sugar into his coffee, while unbeknownst to him, his youngest sister, whose shift at the coffee shop started an hour ago, is being carted to the morgue. He is so tired when he sits at one of the tables that he can feel the loose skin stretching over his eye sockets like wet denim. He watches a boy of about two play with tinker toys on foam mats while his mother reads a 2007 issue of Cosmo. Soon Ella will be that age. He thinks back to the diorama he is making for Margot's youngest, and to the phone conversation the afternoon before. She was 16 weeks and it was going to be a girl. Her name would be Dessa, short for Desdemona, and she was excited. Margot felt that Dessa would be the heroine of the family, for some reason. Teddy feels crumbs in the pocket of his coat, thinks he should call his other sisters to arrange a brunch or something. His phone rings. It's Matthew, his brother-in-law. Teddy lets it go to voicemail and types out a text message to his girlfriend. He deletes it and types a new message. His phone beeps, it's Matthew. He ignores it, instead opening up an app where he can browse images and their sources. He types in *Fitcher's Bird* and "taxidermy" for inspiration. He shudders and stifles a laugh. Just pictures of 1970s clowns. Teddy tries "taxidermy + fairy tales." Better. The taxidermy world is shrinking in some ways, and growing in others. Textile artists have caught on to its resurgence in popularity, felting animal heads and mounting them like trophies. Painters reimagine classic paintings with cats instead of Marie Antoinette. *This is not taxidermy,* Teddy thinks. *This is bullshit PETA-meets-etsy-hipster-millenial-instagram nonsense.* This doesn't stop Teddy from scrolling through the feed of whimsical dioramas on his phone while he sips his Americano, looking for inspiration for his latest project. *Fitcher's Bird,* his favourite tale from the Brother's Grimm. He will make a diorama of the final scene, in which the youngest sister of three rescues and rebuilds her dismembered sisters from a murderous beggar. A small girl stares at Teddy from one of the other tables.

"Daddy," she says, staring at Teddy, "Why is that man so milky?" The father glances up from his coffee and shrugs.

"Everyone is different, sweetie,"

"But he's like, really milky, —or like snow that doesn't have mud on it!"

"That's Teddy Morris, he's an albino."

"What's that, daddy?"

"It means he doesn't have a lot of colour in his skin."

Teddy smiles, listening to the hushed voices. The girl reminds him of his nieces. He slips both of his hands around his coffee mug, his long fingers grazing the rough edges of the pottery. Teddy runs his hands through his long hair, wipes a dribble of coffee out of his beard. Sighing, he drinks the rest of his coffee quickly and leaves, his mind fixed on the diorama and *Fitcher's Bird.*

CHAPTER 4

When they officially announce Margot Morris' death at the bee meeting, there is nobody to take notes. She has been the secretary for all five years, and now the secretary is gone, and with her the will to remember the Bee Meetings. Margot took diligent notes through every other tragedy in the Valley.

She took notes when Carson, the old man who was a permanent fixture at the coffee shop, died in his chair by the window. The baristas closed over Christmas without noticing the old man in his death sleep, and left him there for two nights. She took notes when the Thompson girl drowned in the river by the gas plant. and when Agatha had her stillborn twins.

Margot took notes when Agatha had her stillborn twins.

Margot Morris sat calmly at the end of the table and took notes through every up and down the Valley saw. Now that she is gone, the other members of the committee whisper, as if they no longer know how to talk now that their words aren't being recorded.

"I heard they were already dead when the fire started."

"I knew she was pregnant, I bet that's why he killed her."

"To kill the children too, though? How awful."

"The whole thing is just absolutely devastating."

"Two children, an unborn baby, and a mother."

"They haven't released a cause of death yet."

"I heard the fire barely touched her."

"I heard that something was … off about the crime scene."

"Obviously, I mean three and a half people are dead."

"Ingrid, you can't say that!"

"Say what? Three and a half? Well the baby wasn't born yet. I know, it's just… "Maybe she wasn't even going to keep it!"

Agatha stares at her hands.

"Okay, everyone," Agatha clears her throat. The others look at her, bug-eyed, as though they have forgotten that the sister of the subject of their gossip is among them, "Back to business. Ingrid, can you please take notes? You can take them on your phone, that's fine. Now, obviously I am devastated about the death of my sister and nieces, but right now I really need you all to focus on the garden and the hives. We need someone to collect and dry wild sage for the herbed honey. Matthew, you can wait until next month to present your report on recent bat activity. Same with Ingrid and Tasia and your report on the hummingbird activity east of the Valley."

"Matthew, where is Sylvia?" a woman named Christie asks,

"Ingrid, please," Agatha says, breathing in sharply and clicking her tongue, "Let's get back to the meeting. We've all had enough emotions for today. My sister would want us to keep going with the meeting. This week I am planting Oleanders, Monkshood, Foxglove, and Nightshade, as well as a variety of other bee-friendly plants. Any volunteers to help?"

Tim Gleason raises his hand, drumming his fingers on the table. "Thanks, Tim…"

"Aggie. Slow down," Matthew reaches a hand across the table to touch his sister-in-law's. Agatha jerks it away and continues.

"The butterfly boxes were knocked out of the trees during last night's hail storm. We need one or two volunteers to put them back up. Our rhubarb cordial did very well at the market last Saturday, we sold out by noon. Next week…"

"Sorry to cut you off, Agatha, but I really think we need to suspend meetings for a few weeks so that we can prepare for the funeral."

"Matthew." Agatha glares razor blades at her brother-in-law, "We've got to keep going. Not only is it the most fertile time of year, but I think it is best to keep busy. In fact, I *know* it's best to keep busy in times of loss. Believe me, this is not the first loss in my life, or my siblings' lives." The others at the table avoid eye contact, and Agatha peers at them over her glasses, appearing much older than she is. She is normally very attractive—slim, dark-featured, with a perpetual smirk, but now she is always inhaling through her nose, the nostrils constricting as she grinds her teeth and her eyelashes hit the top of her frames, blinking too often.

"Aggie, Matt. It's okay," Teddy's girlfriend, Tasia, bows her head when she enters the conversation, "Teddy and I are willing to do anything we can to help…"

"Of course you are! He's her fucking brother!" Agatha is shaking now, she's knocked over a glass of water. Tim Gleason jumps to his feet.

"I'll go get a towel," he hurries into the kitchen of the coffee shop. Matthew stands up and walks over to Agatha, placing his hands on her shoulders. She tries to shrug them off at first, but gives in.

"Perhaps it is best if we adjourn for now," Agatha says slowly, breathing deeply, coming back to herself.

Matthew smiles, "Let's head back to mine. Syl is at home with Ella, we can order takeout."

"I'll call Ted to meet us there," Tasia says, "Can I drive you, Ag?"

"I'm not really up for—well, fine. I'd like to see Ella."

"Ted's on his way to yours, Matt."

"We'll see you back at mine, then." Matthew wraps Agatha into a one-armed hug, kissing her on the cheek.

Tim Gleeson watched the family members walk out of the coffee shop before sitting back down at the table with the others.

"Well, fuck."

"I mean, the whole family is a bit nuts, right?"

"It's called grief, Ingrid."

"No, not just now! I mean they've always been a bit nuts."

"Tasia and Matthew aren't really related."

"Well, Agatha is nuts, we all know that."

"Damn good gardener, though."

"Used to be a good midwife, too."

"Wonder if her husband will be at the funeral."

"I thought they were getting divorced?"

"They are."

"Where's Ted, today?"

"Funeral shit, probably. It's gonna be a big one."

The Morrises and their respective spouses were always a topic of local gossip. Some people in the town resented them. Agatha and Sylvia, tall and angular, were always mocked for dressing "like they were better than the Valley."

"They dress like they live in Toronto," people would whisper, glaring at their long black dresses and gauzy shawls. Many people in the town were afraid of Teddy, for his albinism, or maybe his natural gift with dead animals. They resented that women liked him, despite his lack of pigment, that his monochrome body was desirable, that his difference was strangely beautiful. Agatha's string of miscarriages and failed marriages seemed like a curse, and Sylvia's sinewy muscle and unladylike pursuits–. Margot was well-liked, but her status as an overweight single mother brought more condescending pity than admiration.

***

Sylvia does sets of 32 pull-ups. 31 pull-ups for 31 years and one for the year with Ella, because it feels she's aged twice as fast since the baby was born. The infant bounces in her chair, watching her mother hang from the door frame. Some children's song plays and Ella is maybe dancing to it, or she is bored and knows her mother isn't one for affection. Who knows the thoughts of a baby? One hundred and twelve push-ups; the sum of the her and her siblings' ages. Ella cries and Sylvia glances over at her before running to the kitchen.

"I'll be right there," she mumbles, running the tap until the water is hot. She rolls a bottle of formula under it. Ella screams. Sylvia thrusts the bottle at the child. Ella screams louder. Sylvia forgot to test the formula on her wrist. She is glad no one is home to see her burn her baby's mouth. She removes the bottle and tests it on her wrist. A kitten runs underfoot.

Jesus Christ, I should have drowned them like I'd planned. She pops the bottle in Ella's mouth, holding her breath while the infant takes the nipple. When all is calm, she goes back to her exercises. Thirty-seven pull-ups, one for each year of her husband's life.

Sylvia feels too old to be the mother of an infant, but she also feels too young to be at home with said infant when she could be climbing. She notices that the same children's song has been on repeat for god knows how long and so she turns the stereo off.

"Miss Ella, I think it's time for a walk and a coffee," Say what you will about Sylvia Morris' parenting: she gets the kid outside a lot.

Sylvia orders a triple espresso, and watches as the barista– a teenager with chunky black glasses– packs the shot. He scrapes the excess grounds away from the puck and firmly tamps it. She watches the caramel colour run down the side of the small mug, the crema swirling over top of the hot black liquid. She shakes a packet of brown sugar and glances over her shoulder to make sure Ella is still in her stroller at the table. The child sleeps, comforted by the noise of the coffee grinder. The barista smiles at Sylvia and hands her the espresso. She places it on the counter and shakes the brown sugar over top. It immediately sinks through the crema. She tells the barista to try again, and again, and again after that, until the crema is a membrane through which sweetness cannot seep. Her phone beeps. *Everyone's coming over for takeout. See you around 5?*

***

Agatha goes to the Valley Hotel and Bar after eating takeout from Happy Valley with her family. She smears beeswax on her lips. She comes here when she's restless. She does the same play that she did as a student at Mount Royal University. If you want to sleep with someone, ask for a drag of their cigarette, in the dim light of nightfall, on an unfamiliar porch. Agatha doesn't smoke much anymore, except for these restless days. Make sure that the light is soft, and falls lightly on your eyelashes, which should be thick with kohl. It is summer and Agatha is twenty-seven and not nineteen, so she washes the dirt from her nails and wears a loose tank top. A drag, someone once told Agatha, when she was sixteen, maybe, is three long inhales. Enough time to scope someone out entirely. Look at them through your lashes, heavy with snowflakes or the dust of summer, while you breathe in. Suck on your cheeks, and let the corners of your eyes crinkle. Make sure that you can feel the soft tissue of your cheeks between your back molars. It is important to bite your cheeks on unfamiliar porches, or the too-familiar front steps of the only bar in town. Scrunch your eyes so that they become moist, but not like you're about to cry. Make them look pained, but beautiful. Like a dead, but still intact moth. Like the fifteen- no-sixteen dead queens above Agatha's bed. Blow the smoke out in a line, just below their chin and to the left. Hand their cigarette back, through soft fingers that linger next to theirs. Say ambivalent, soft things, and blink the snowflakes or dust off of your eyelashes on that unfamiliar porch or familiar step. Shuffle closer to them in the cold, or in the heat. They may be taken aback by you, so ask for a cigarette of your own and talk about how when your heart is broken you listen to Joy Division in the dark, in a scalding hot bath, like a teenager. Agatha knows she is no longer nineteen. She is old enough–and looks it–that she will be expected to talk about family, career, household affairs. Talk about your nieces (Your *niece*—there is only one now). Talk about how you lived in Amsterdam for a year after your first divorce. Talk about how the divorce was your idea. It's probably best not to mention the taxidermy duck on your bedside table, the dead queens that watch over you while you sleep, or who your ex is– it's a small town, after all, and if they don't already know who you are, why tell them?

Agatha think that the hives are a safe subject, and maybe the sunflowers that grow to 8 feet tall every year though no one has ever planted any. Balance the erotic with the neurotic. Talk about the new vibrator you just bought, and in the same breath mention that your mother died ten years ago, in a freak accident involving a bucking horse and an old red barn. Make them want to save you while they touch you in the bathroom of the too familiar bar. Agatha listens to her younger self, instead of the man standing across from her. Her head is filled with her own voice and the insects laid out on her desk, ready to find resin or frames.

When you are nearing the end of your cigarette, inch closer to him with every second exhale. Look down as you stamp the embers into the pavement. When you look up, find his lips with yours, and linger. Let his hands find their way to your face. He will probably tuck a hair behind your ear or touch your lower back. You are still boney enough to pass for a woman who doesn't know what she wants. *In twelve hours, I can install the new queen.* If he finds a coin behind your ear, it is up to you but you may want to leave. This tends to happen in the Valley: magicians roll into town after tragedies.

The old queen's long, thin belly quivered for a moment after she died. Margot's long, thin belly probably did, too. Laugh breathlessly and touch your forehead to his chin. "Sorry," you'll say, "I don't know what got into me." Your apology will make him feel as though he is in charge. Find his fingers and entwine them with yours. Look him dead in the eyes and say, "Should we?" then look away. *The tallest sunflower was a bit wilted this morning, its head too heavy for its body. Like a newborn. Like Margot's unborn baby.* Kiss him softly on the neck, and guide him back into the bar or out to your car, or into the alleyway. When you were nineteen, you would lead him through a crowded party, thinking that your night was better than everyone else's. You wouldn't make eye contact with him, just lead the way up the narrow stairs with the blank white walls, to a bedroom that smells of peach flavored cigars and printer ink.

Now, Agatha stares past a man's eyes. He mistakes this for seductive eye contact and kisses her. With his tongue in her mouth Agatha will wonder if she remembered to clean out the hummingbird feeder. From above you look like maggots squirming. Your legs become tangled in the sheets of the bed with a stranger's scent on them, but to the sheets you are the stranger. He will move slowly on top of you, and his weight will feel pleasant. Maybe not comfortable; your heart will not race like it did when you slept with your college boyfriend, but it will be pleasant. Twenty-seven-year-old Agatha and nineteen-year-old Agatha have different ideas on how the night will end. Agatha excuses herself to the bathroom and leaves. There are insects to pin, birds to feed, and a funeral to plan. A triple funeral. A Russian Nesting Doll funeral.

***

Sylvia was with Agatha when she went to identify the bodies. They sat in the morgue, blood pooling to the bottom of the corpses so that they looked like layer cakes, bright white on top and red at the bottom. Margot's blue eyes were crawling with maggots and her fingernails were turning black. Sylvia vomited in a nearby garbage can, sobbing, while Agatha filled out the forms. On the drive home, Sylvia wouldn't speak, her face a smooth stone once again.

CHAPTER 5

Teddy lies on his stomach on the bed, two books open in front of him. He and Tasia have just returned from the library. She is on the couch doing crosswords. Her toes balance on the bed, her legs bridging the foot between the two. Teddy can see the Agatha's hives through the window. The converted Atco trailer that he and Tasia live in is illegally parked on Agatha's property, but the town has never made a fuss.

In an attempt to help out Agatha, he is reading a book about bees. In an attempt to prepare himself to see Margot and the girls, he is reading a book about morticians.

Agatha mentioned something about swarms. *It's swarm season, Ted.* The book says this:

"It is advisable to attend at least one seminar with an experienced Swarm Catcher before trying it on your own. You are going to need protective garments like a veil and a jacket."

He sighs and looks over at the other book, open to page 43: *Makeup Techniques for Morticians.*

"The amount of makeup that is applied depends on the condition of the body. Makeup will be applied to the face, neck, and hands in order to make the person look as alive as possible and cover up any blemishes, discolouration, or marks of illness."

Though Teddy deals with dead animals for a living, he begged his sisters to identify Margot's body without him. *Marks of illness? Maybe Margot and the girls were ill. Some weird disease. Some disease contained to that single wing of their home.*

"For a few dollars extra, you can have your queen marked." Teddy forgets which book he is reading and wonders why the mortician's book is talking about bees.

"Lots of enthusiasts come across swarms. You can get them off of Craigslist or just check for forums in your area." Teddy wonders if the book is telling him to get swarms of bees off of Craigslist, or the bee enthusiasts.

"If the person who died wore a wig or toupee, the mortician has a much easier job with styling, so long as it remains intact or a similar one can be ordered. In cases where the body suffered from a degenerative illness or an injurious accident, cosmetic reconstruction may be necessary." Teddy wonders if his sister will need cosmetic surgery, or his nieces. Probably some heavy makeup for the burns, or maybe they will be put in pants?

"Bee swarms prefer standing water with natural minerals. You also need a container source of some sort, but nothing fancy." Teddy shudders, thinking of the funeral. Talk about a swarm. All those well-meaning people with their black pants and dresses staring at him with tears in their eyes.

"Undertakers can do most anything: reattaching heads, sewing up gunshot wounds, waxing over burns." At least he knows his sister and her daughters were not decapitated. The books blur together as Teddy's eyes grow heavy with the fever of the last two days.

"Use a smoker—a little firebox and bellow rig."

"Don't forget to sweep out the metal."

"The stingers will be gone."

"Before grinding the bones."

His phone beeps. A news alert he set up to try to connect with Sylvia. *Mother of two children among six mountaineers presumed dead after failed expedition.*

***

When Teddy wakes, he cannot add up the numbers on the clock to figure out what time it is. The room is darker, colder, and the pages of the book he fell asleep on stick to his forehead. Tasia snores softly on the couch. His back aches from sleeping on his stomach. He shoves the two library books off of the bed and sits up, resting his head in his hands. He yawns, and reaches for a pack of cigarettes on the bedside table. He lights one and inhales. He reaches for his copy of Grimm's Fairy tales on the bedside table. Opening to *Fitcher's Bird*, he flicks ash into a tray.

"There was a sorcerer who disguised himself as a beggar in order to appear harmless. He walked with a limp and carried a sack, in order to look destitute. He went from house to house under the guise of begging in order to steal young girls away. If he touched them, they were compelled to jump into his sack and they were never seen again. Nobody knew where he took them or what happened to them.

One day, he went to the home of a man who had three daughters. The daughters were known for their beauty and youth. He knocked at the door, asking for something to eat. The eldest daughter came out with a loaf of bread she had made. He gripped her hand in thanks, and the girl was compelled to jump into his sack.

He took the girl back to his home, where he told her she was to be his wife. The house was beautiful and the sorcerer assured the girl that she would be happy and that he would do anything for her.

"Now, my darling. I must go away for a day. Stay here. You may explore the house and go anywhere except for the room at the back, behind the kitchen. If you enter it, I will make sure that you are killed. Here, keep this egg with you at all times. If any harm befalls the egg, more harm will befall you." He gave the girl a pristine white egg, and left. Of course, the girl's curiosity got to her after she tired of reading and staring at the egg, and she snuck towards the forbidden room. Inside were porcelain tubs full of blood and body parts. Shocked, she dropped the egg. It did not break, but it rolled on the floor and became covered in blood. The girl tried and tried to rinse the blood off of the egg, to no avail.

When the sorcerer came home that night, he found the girl weeping, cradling the bloody egg in her arms. Furious and certain of her transgressions, he took her into the room with the bodies and dismembered her, too. Placing her assorted limbs in different tubs.

The next day, the man went back to the girl's home, and returned with the middle sister. The same fate befell her as did her elder sister. Again, he went away for a day to test the girl. Again, he gave her an egg and forbid her to enter the back room. Again, curiosity led the girl to the room where she dropped the egg. Again, the egg rolled in the blood, and again, the sorcerer dismembered the girl for her sins.

The man returned to the home, hoping that the youngest girl would obey him. He touched her hand and she jumped into his sack. He took her back to his home and promised her a life of luxury. The youngest sister, however, had watched her older sisters disappear, and was suspicious of the man. She, too, was curious about the room, but she wisely left the egg outside as she crept inside. She saw her murdered sisters in bits and pieces. In her grief, she collected the bits of her sisters and placed them on the floor in the proper order. She wept over their bodies until the limbs began to quiver and come together, crudely reassembling themselves. The sisters opened their eyes, coming back to life. They cried and hugged their little sister. The youngest sister knew that the man would return soon, so she drew a bath and scrubbed herself clean of all the blood, telling her sisters to hide in the closet until she signaled for them to come out.

When the man returned and saw that the egg was still pristine, he said "You have passed the test. Now you are to be my bride!" He now had to do whatever the youngest sister demanded.

"I will make wedding preparations and you must carry a basket of gold to my parents." In the basket, she hid her sisters under the gold and told the sorcerer to take it to her parents. In his absence, she found a skull and adorned it with jewels and a wig to look lifelike, and placed it in the window to look like she was looking out. She then covered herself with honey and tore open the bed, covering herself in feathers. She hid in a tree, disguised as a bird, and watched as the man returned to wave at the skull, thinking it to be his bride. He walked up to join her, but before he reached the doorstep, the sisters' family arrived and beat the sorcerer to death."

Teddy knows the story so well that he recites it in his head, staring at the pages of the book, the small black and white illustrations. Three sisters. Sylvia, Agatha, Margot. Three sisters. Luna, Lola, and the baby. Who was left to put Sylvia and Agatha back together? Why couldn't the baby and the sheer matter of her not yet fully existing, save his nieces?

Teddy lights another cigarette and picks up the book on morticians again:

"The undertaker slips plastic caps under the eyelids to keep them shut– sharp ridges dig into the lids so that they do not spring open in front of grieving relatives. The jaw is wired shut, up through the septum, so that it stays still and doesn't gape open. The undertaker stuffs cotton in all orifices: nose, anus, and vagina, to prevent leakage." He flips to another page:

"The embalmer will massage the body's limbs, stiff from rigor mortis."

Not so different from taxidermy, thinks Teddy. He decides that the diorama will be of three voles: the two reassembled sisters below a tree, looking up at the youngest in the tree, covered with feathers.

***

"They were found over there. The bodies, I mean," Agatha gestures towards the remains of a doorway. All that is left in the room is the blackened skeleton of a metal bed frame. Agatha enters slowly, Sylvia holds tight to her coat, and Teddy follows, his hands resting gingerly on Sylvia's hunched shoulders.

"Fuck," Sylvia chews on her sleeve. The room smells like fire and chemicals.

Teddy shifts from his left foot to his right. "I just can't believe they haven't figured out how it happened—what—who did it." Agatha fumbles for Teddy's hand. The three stand in the rotting carcass that was their sister's home. Sylvia leans into Agatha. A police officer stands back from them, staring intently at the floor.

"I miss her. I just really fucking miss her, Aggie." Sylvia inhales loudly.

Teddy squeezes Agatha's hand and turns to embrace his sisters.

"Like, she died here, in this room. With her babies. Her fucking children. They died together, here. How?" Sylvia sobs into Teddy's chest. Agatha breaks away and walks to the edge of the bed. She grips a bedpost. The ragged springs from the burnt mattress are black ringlets scattered on the floor.

"Margot," she whispers, "I'm so sorry." She nudges the soot with her foot. Agatha blinks back tears. The ashes spread around the room like tea leaves. Dark stains spread on the floor like inkblots. On the other side of the bed, chalk outlines indicate the placement of the bodies. Three outlines. In order of largest to smallest. So deliberately placed. So calm. So… eerie.

Teddy kneels next to them, his fingers nearly touching the chalk dust. Sylvia backs towards the door, eyes fixed on the outlines.

"I just, I don't want to be here anymore, sorry, guys." Sylvia stumbles over broken wood and ash to walk quickly out of the bedroom. Agatha squeezes Teddy's shoulder and follows her sister. She brushes past the officer on the way out. He stares at his phone, leaning against the wall. Anger flushes into Agatha's body. Even though she knows it's his first week, that he's new, in this moment she hates this police officer. She hates his hunched shoulders pressed against her sister's blackened wall. His shape will stay there, an imprint in the soot. She hates him for letting them into their dead sister's house. For not cleaning up the chalk outlines. For not having any answers. For playing Candy Crush on his phone while her brother kneels unmoving where the bodies were found. For responding to texts while her sister ran off somewhere to cry or be alone or compose herself or call her husband. The police officer starts, feeling her eyes on him. He shoves his phone into his pocket.

"I–I'm sorry, miss. I am, really. Just give me a shout when you're ready to go. I–I'm sorry."

Agatha wanders into Margot's living room. She stares at the photos on the mantle. Family portraits of Margot and her daughters, Sylvia and Matthew's wedding. Ella's birth. A polaroid of Teddy and Tasia kissing, wearing New Year's Eve hats. Agatha at the local farmer's market in a straw hat, holding up two jars of honey. Her first sale. Tucked behind Margot's high school graduation portrait is a yellowed photo, curling in on itself as if it wants to hide. In it, Margot's head is thrown back, Sylvia grins sheepishly, Teddy stares out the window, and Agatha's mouth is wide open, mid-sentence. They are huddled together on their parents' bed, Agatha reading from *Grimm's Fairy Tales*. Margot holds their cat, Silas, in her lap. Agatha wishes she could retell all of those childhood stories. That she could warn her siblings of the heartache of growing up. That they could have stayed cocooned in the purple comforter of their parents' bed, where they found themselves all huddled on cold winter nights. Six people crammed into the bed with Silas sitting triumphant on top of the covers, purring. Agatha wanted to rewrite the stories, that already warned them with their headless women and evil men, to keep her family safe.

Once upon a time it was not safe to be born a girl. It is important to remember that time does not exist. Once upon a time, all of time, it was not safe to be a girl. Lecherous men would disguise themselves as kittens left for dead by their mothers so that little girls would pick them up and kiss their eyes into vision and then the kittens would grow and grow until they were bigger and fiercer than lions and they would eat the girls in one bite, bones and skin and hair and all. Once upon a time it was not safe to be born a girl because either you were the kitten abandoned in a dumpster or you were devoured by it. Once upon a time it was not safe to be a girl because girls have fires inside of them and men who are cold cling to their warmth until they leech it from the bones of women and then burn them to death with their own matches.

CHAPTER 6

"Bee mating happens outside of the hive in mid-flight, 200 to 300 feet in the air and usually a mile or more away from home. The drone's big eyes are handy for spotting virgin queens taking what are called 'nuptial flights.' The real trick is to get the queen, because the rest of the swarm will gather around her." Agatha pulls weeds as she listens to a new audiobook she's downloaded. *The Modern Beekeeper: A Guide to Keeping and Caring for you Home Apiary.* It is the morning of the funeral. Agatha is determined to keep this hive alive over the winter. Agatha is determined to keep something alive.

Six years after her mother's death, the bees had taken over Agatha's childhood home, or *Istria*, as her mother had called it. Sylvia and Margot had families to look after, and Teddy was busy with the taxidermy shop, so nobody had been looking after the house. It was late August and out of the attic door in the ceiling spilled an enormous colony of bees. The colony reached for the shag carpet like a giant, melting stalactite. Agatha gagged upon seeing it. The buzzing was unbearable, and the bees coated the greenish hive like black mold; a quivering, humming black mold. In Margot's old bedroom sat Silas, the stuffed family cat, somehow ripped open at the stomach seam. From his waxy wounds poured more honeycombs. Bees crawled out of the creature's eyes and around his large, bat-like ears. Coming home from her broken career as a midwife and her fourth broken marriage was less comforting than expected. Everywhere she went she was haunted by newborns crawling out of dead things. The entire earth felt more fertile than she did. Over four months—well into December—Agatha had the bees and the mice removed, the wood paneling re-done, the shag carpet torn out and the beams reinforced. She then moved her things into Istria. She piled the remnants of her four marriages in a closet, stacked the paperwork and books from her failed career on an old table in the attic, and settled into a quiet, solitary life, like a Hairy Footed Flower Bee.

Agatha examines herself in the long mirror. It was her mother's. The room is almost identical to the way her mother kept it; the mattress creaking in the frame, the linens yellowing in the sun that slips through the large, drafty windows. The draft snakes that she and her sisters sewed one windy winter still sit along the windowsills, faded pink bargain-bin fabric in long tubes and tied with tacky scalloped ribbons. She rubs at the dots of calamine lotion all along her arms, blending the pink paint into her skin to reveal a series of bee stings.

Agatha's left elbow is dry and hairy. She scratches at a particularly large sting on the tip. She feels she is going to scratch through to bone before leaving the house. Her old midwifery books lay scattered on the bed and the floor. She must have opened them after drinking last night. Agatha leans down and reads the first sentence that catches her eye:

"The dead birth is often easier than a live birth; inexperienced midwives and even pathologists and mortuary workers have been able to facilitate the birth without trouble." Agatha laughs. Of course it is easy to pull a dead infant out of a dead woman when it is already being expelled by decomposition.

Her black dress, once her aunt's, is done up in the back with mustard loop-buttons, crawling up her spine like the round bottoms of bumblebees. With no one to do it up for her, she buttons it three quarters of the way before tugging it over her head and contorting her shoulders to reach the top buttons. She digs in her jewelry box for the necklace her mother gave her: a queen bee in a bubble of resin glued to an ornate round frame, and hung on a long brass chain.

Agatha gathers the books and shoves them into the wardrobe. She grabs her purse and her stockings. She stretches them over her legs, her short, sharp hairs poking through the nylon. They sag around the ankles. There is a tear exposing her sharp left hipbone. She doesn't have time to run to the drugstore and buy a new pair. Agatha crawls onto her bed, kissing the dead queens above it, one after the other.

***

The photo is of his family: Sylvia, him, Agatha, Margot, and their parents. They stand in front of a Christmas tree. The women all wear red shift dresses. Teddy and his father wear gray suits with red ties. The women wear matching necklaces; queen bees cast in resin. Their mother wears her Victorian hummingbird earrings, a violent blue. Teddy and his father wear cufflinks: resin with worker bees in them. There were no kings or princes in their household, only queens and workers. Still, the photo brings a smile to Teddy's face. Father's crimson eyes match mother's dress. Teddy holds Louis, his first creation, proudly up to his chin. The girls squirm with mischief, making them slightly blurred. Their parents have an easy loftiness. The family cat, a fat hairless thing, skulks at their feet. Most of the Morris family photos were elaborate, staged affairs. Lulu, their mother, would dress them in outfits that contrasted with the alabaster men and murky women. Usually this meant that the women wore red to reflect the eyes of the men, or black to match their own curtains of hair. Sometimes, in the summer, they wore vibrant colours: mustard, indigo, violet. Always block colours, always painfully visible next to the men. This photo is different: an outtake. One he found in a box in Istria's attic.

Teddy knows he should be getting ready for the funeral. His youngest sister and his nieces are to be tucked away. Agatha called him the night before.

"I saw the bodies," she whispered. "I saw Margot. I saw the baby. She was like mercury, like you and dad. Like thin milk. She was like you and dad." He hung up the phone without saying a word, and went to bed.

Teddy looks back at the photo of his family. It is the only one he displays in his and Tasia's trailer, hung over the sofa, above a small shelf that holds several knick-knacks. Louis is there, along with a cigarette tin of mismatched glass eyes that his father used to keep in the car. When Teddy would climb into the Volvo, his father would say; *Taxidermists should always keep the eyes they don't use. For good luck, and for emergencies.* Casper Morris was a commanding man for how little pigment he possessed.

Louis was older than all of Teddy's nieces. Louis was a field mouse that Teddy's father found in the garden shed one Sunday in January, circled by raven feathers, like a sun. Teddy suspected Margot had arranged them as a tribute, but his youngest sister barely talked in those days.

Louis wasn't a great example of Morris Family Taxidermy. His fur was more matted after his grooming than it had been when he was found in the shed. His eyes were two different sizes and colours, because Sylvia thought he looked more interesting that way. They bulged, for Teddy had mistakenly used otter eyes instead of the small black beads used for mice. Louis wore a tiny tweed suit that Agatha and their mother sewed from scraps they found in the attic. The glue around his mouth made him look a bit like he had rabies, and there was a mess of glittery pink nail polish on his claws from when he disappeared into Margot's room for a 'pyjama party.' Louis' crooked smile and squashed nose made him look more constipated than the usual stuffed mouse. Still, Teddy loves him enough to display the mouse in his home. As a child, he loved the workshop that smelled of glue, oak, preservatives, and dead animals. He loved the way his father had bit his lower lip while stuffing a tiny animal with tweezers full of cotton batting. Even now, he loves thinking back to his father haphazardly supervising the preservation of this mouse while working on a gopher.

Teddy grins at the memory of his father's white lips filling with blood in his workshop. Teddy spent hours watching his father carefully prepare specimens—mostly fish and small game for local hunters. But, in the spring of 1996, 10-year-old Teddy watched his father stuff gopher after gopher, dressing them in outfits and creating dioramas for the Toddington Gopher Hole museum, which was set to open the following year. This was much more interesting than the deer heads Teddy saw over and over. This, he thought, was art.

Teddy digs a gray suit out from the back of his closet, last worn at his mother's funeral. He fishes his cufflinks out of a drawer in the kitchen. Worker bees. Twin worker bees, rounder than his sisters' queens. Prettier, he thinks. They are visibly fuzzy and a brighter hue of yellow.

***

With low expectations, Sylvia takes a file to her nails. Jagged, short, and torn at the cuticles, they refuse to look 'proper.' The right ring finger nail has a black dot that is nearly half grown out, about the size of a pea. Her left pinky nail is almost entirely gone. Both of her thumbs have bright pink strips of new skin sticking out from the sides. The white dust from the file floats onto her black nylons. *It looks like chalk*, she thinks, scratching at the remnants of a blister on her palm. Her nylons creep over her belly and she tugs at the small strip of fat that snuck over the line of her underwear, over the crevice in her stomach.

Before the pregnancy, Sylvia was climbing routes with a grade of 5.11 no problem. Now, a year and a half later, she struggles to climb a 5.9. 5.10 is her next goal, to be completed as soon as the bodies are burnt and the family calmed. She wants—no, needs to climb. Needs something. She was feeling restless before the deaths, but now, she needs to feel something other than the stale heft of death that follows her.

Sylvia tugs a black pantsuit over her legs. It is chic and tight, showing off her toned arms. Her husband comes into the room wearing a dress shirt and pink boxers, Ella in his arms, wearing a pink onesie that said 'Take me to the Mountains.' Ella is covered in something brown that is also strewn across Matthew's white pressed shirt. Sylvia glances at her husband and bursts into laughter. She continues to laugh as the stunned infant looks back and forth between her parents, Matthew looking disgruntled and bewildered and Sylvia gasping for air between belly-laughs.

"Last time we buy the organic porridge," she says, pointing at the en-suite bathroom. "We have to leave in twenty minutes, you two get cleaned up." She rubs at her eyes and grabs her necklace off of the dresser.

"Queen bees for my little ladies," her mother used to say. "Selfless, ruthless, and life-giving." Ella babbles away at Matthew, who chuckles as he cleans himself and the child. Sylvia smiles. *He really is a great father,* she thinks, brushing off earlier doubts and agonies.

***

The skin on Margot Morris' calves and feet boiled in the fire, somehow. *Bacon-wrapped bones,* thought the undertaker, as he put on his goggles to protect from potential splashes. His cigarette sat in an ashtray by Margot's head. He stuck his hand into the wax, and began molding the woman's calves smooth. She used to be such a pretty girl, he thought, remembering how she worked at the coffee shop through high school. She was the friendliest Morris girl, her kindness accentuated by the blunt bangs that made her face appear rounder, less sharp than her sisters and mother.

Yes, Margot Morris was a good egg. Even though she had two— well, three now—children from different fathers, she was sweet and the right sort of plump. Friendly plump. She was accessible. She let the town into the cocoon of the Morrises. Her daughters were very sweet, too, taking after their mother. The eldest one was tall like her aunts and uncle, and the younger one was shorter, like her mother, and cheery where her sister could be sullen. The new baby had begun to show signs of the albinism that plagued Teddy and his father, Casper Morris.

The undertaker was no stranger to Morris family funerals. He had cremated three of Agatha's stillborn babies—a yearly affair in the early 2010s—and he had also been the one to dress up the infamous matriarch one last time. It was Morris family custom for the deceased woman to wear Great Aunt Theodosia's hummingbird earrings at the funeral, which was to be an open casket. Theodosia was Casper's eccentric aunt, and she left Lulu the earrings in her will. It was rumoured that the old woman was Casper's birth mother, but could not raise him as she was only 14 when she became pregnant. This was just old town gossip and ghost stories, though. Theodosia was a sweet woman, a real fixture in the community, even if she looked a bit like Queen Vicky in her later days.

The Moth and Cradle Funeral Home had seen an increase in revenue in the last few years, with the increasing popularity of the death positivity movement, and the appearance of Death Doulas in the Valley. People came from as far as Calgary for their 'Old world charm' and 'Bohemian flair.' The undertaker prided himself on urns imported from all over the world and offered burial and cremation rituals from various cultures. At the time of Margot Morris' death, the trend was a traditional Japanese cremation, where the relatives watched the undertaker slide the body (much more carefully than he would if he were alone) into the cremation chamber. Hours later, once the organic matter had melted off, and all of the body's moisture evaporated, they would take chopsticks (the undertaker bought them from a dollar store in Okotoks) and gently place each bone starting at the feet into a turquoise urn from Morocco. The last funeral that the undertaker witnessed concluded in a flash mob of *Closing Time* by Semisonic.

CHAPTER 7

Margot lays in the casket, lips pursed into a near-smile, with three other caskets decreasing in size next to her. The smallest casket is closed but the others are open, revealing two girls in white dresses, their hair in golden ringlets and lips and cheeks flushed with pink. They look as though the funeral director took a white-out marker to their freckles. Agatha wonders why the girls are dressed and positioned like china dolls. It is unnerving, she thinks, the way they lay still in their square boxes. She half expects a small metal stand to lay beneath them, so that they can be propped up at a tea party with giant teddy bears and plastic scones. More unsettling, still, are the blue eyes painted over their closed eyelids. A Morris tradition, just like the earrings made from dead birds. The girls, her nieces, are drained of blood. Luna, the eldest, played hockey on the boys' team, and recently cut off her jet-black hair with a pair of her sister's safety scissors. Lola, her younger sister, wore thick round glasses without lenses and had a bright pink streak in her ash blonde hair. The undertaker had placed wigs on their heads and caked their small faces with white makeup. The undertaker had at least left Margot mostly alone, aside from the garishly painted-on eyes. Her freckles, like pollen, sit on her face, dusting her translucent skin with brown and gold.

During the opening sermon, Margot's siblings stand in a line next to the caskets, dressed in shades of black. Sylvia, the eldest, holds her daughter Ella against her hip. Her bicep bulges, curled around the child. Ella sucks on the necklace around Sylvia's neck, her three small teeth rubbing against the resin. She slaps the necklace out of the child's mouth, and gestures to her husband, seating in the front row, to take her. The child wails.

Agatha, the second oldest, but only by ten months, stands next to Sylvia, chewing the skin around her fingernails. She pulls on a loose cuticle and it unravels below her nail, revealing the bloody flesh beneath. She sucks on the blood, staring blankly at the tiny, sealed coffin. Her necklace lays flat against her breastbone. When she shifts her feet it makes an audible clunk against her chest. She feels heat emanate off of Teddy, taking his place between her and the coffins, completing the line of siblings from oldest to youngest.

Agatha scratches at her bee stings. She scratches and scratches until they start bleeding and she is standing in front of a room of people with blood running down her arms and in her mouth where she chewed on her cheek and her cuticle and she is beginning to look deranged. She hears a buzzing and a bee circles her head before landing on her dead sister's brow.

A song begins and everyone in the church stands. *Because* by The Beatles. The bee sitting on Margot's brow twitches, like a dog trying to make a nest in a couch cushion.

The sisters are thin, each in their own way. Margot, in a dead sort of way—she is technically still the chubby sister, Agatha thinks, although death and pallor has brought out her cheekbones. Her neck is slimmer, too. Agatha imagines clothespins behind her sister's throat, holding the loose skin back, the way the hide the excess fabric behind mannequins at stores. Agatha is thin too, but in a living, careless way. Sylvia is thin in a disciplined, verging-on-healthy way. Their black hair, too, is thin. Agatha's is piled on top of her head like a moldy cobweb, or more accurately, like a collapsing beehive. Sylvia's is loose, pulled back from her face. Margot's is spread across her pillow, like Ophelia, but with a noose of hair laid across her neck.

Teddy clears his throat, and the two sisters whip their heads towards him. Their chins slope, pointed and sharp. His eyes widen, and he looks at them, then to Margot. He feels like Margot is also glaring at him in the silence. He can see her sitting up in the coffin and turning her head towards him. He knows that he, too has his mother's sloping, pointed chin, but he can cover his with hair; his sisters' chins jut forwards like knives. Everything about them today is like knives. Their elbows, their eyes, their teeth, their knuckles. Teddy has always been the outlier, the worker bee expelled from the hive. But who wants to get in the way of three queens, anyway?

People whisper in the crowd.

"I thought it was a fire – why aren't they burnt to a crisp?"

"Suffocation, more likely. Or smoke inhalation."

"Undertakers can do wonders with wax, they probably ARE burnt to a crisp."

"Such an odd family. Love-able, but odd."

"Like china dolls–"

"Or porcelain dolls –"

"Russian nesting dolls."

"Why is the fetus in a casket and not in the mother?"

"Coffin birth, maybe?"

"What's that?"

"When the gasses in the abdomen of a corpse push the fetus through the vagina."

"How the hell do you know that?"

"Watched a YouTube video."

"Why?"

"It looked interesting."

"That sounds fake."

"Well, it's rare. It only happens when the body's been left to decompose for a while."

"But the bodies were discovered in like, twelve hours."

"Then I don't know."

***

"My name is Thyme, and I will guide you through this ceremony today. Dearly beloved, friends, family, and colleagues of dear, dear Margot, Lola, and Luna, we are gathered here today to celebrate life, and a bit of death."

The crowd murmurs and the Morris siblings exchange severe looks. The undertaker, standing at the back of the room, fixates on the black tips of his pleather shoes. Yva, the woman who usually officiates Morris funerals, is on vacation in Bermuda with the new barista at the Wayward Coffee Co... She was replaced last minute with Thyme Woelk, a death-doula-in-training.

Thyme's head is shaved on one side in the shape of a star, and she stands at the podium with bright purple lipstick, draped in gauzy black fabric. She is petite, maybe 5'2". She practically drowns in the fabric draped around her. *Like a bloody toddler got into Stevie Nicks' 1977 tour wardrobe,* the undertaker thinks, trying not to wrinkle his nose in distaste.

"Death, my friends, is not the end."

Thyme has a sing-song voice, which seems to float on some extra breath. She reminds the undertaker of a fortune-teller at a fair for children, or someone reciting poetry after doing too many drugs.

"Death is only the beginning of life. Death does not take our loved ones from us, it simply shows them to us in their most natural form." All three living Morris siblings turn around and stare at the undertaker.

"Margot, Luna, and Lola, are all in a better place. A beautiful place. A place where bunnies can eat cotton candy without getting sick, and children never grow up. A Neverland, of sorts. Margot, Luna, and Lola, are with Peter..."

Thyme stops, mid-sentence, looks cross-eyed at a large bee sitting on the bridge of her nose. She stops in horror. There is an audible squeak in the front row, Agatha and Sylvia huddled together, gripping their hands over their mouths and shaking with laughter. The undertaker's eyes widen. Thyme's knuckles whiten, holding onto the podium. Her mouth is a large, purple life-saver. Agatha hiccups loudly, unable to stifle her laugher, and the bee flops from

Thyme's nose, leaving a sting behind. Tears well in her eyes, and she stumbles off the raised platform. The undertaker rushes to the front of the room, and Agatha and Sylvia's laughter falls into the occasional soft chuckle.

"H-hello, everyone." He trips over his words. He has never spoken at a funeral before, though he observes the mourning of every corpse he paints or burns.

"W-Welcome. It is with deepest regrets that we gather here today to celebrate the lives of M-Margot, and her two vibrant daughters." His hands shake.

"M-Most of us remember Margot from her years at Wayward Coffee. She made the best mochas, and she was always ready for a chat when she had to sweep the front of the shop." He starts to get comfortable, and relaxes.

"Those of us in town saw her grow up, from a cheerful girl selling cookies, to a mother of two lovely girls. She joins her mother, Lulu, and her father, Casper, in the afterlife, along with her daughters. These three women were taken too soon and will be missed. In times like this, the true strength of our community shows, as we must not forget them, and must support each other in times of loss. Sylvia, Edward, Agatha– w–would you like to say a few words?"

Agatha gets up first.

"Margot was the baby. I see her lying there, and it reminds me of when Sylvia and I would have sleepovers with our friends, and sneak into her and Teddy's rooms with shaving cream or Sharpie markers. I remember this time, when Margot was five. She found the catnip in the cupboard and fed it to our cat Silas until he stumbled around the house in a drunken stupor before falling asleep in the bathtub. Margot is…was so fun. She enjoyed literally everything. I don't know how, or why, but she was always smiling. It never bothered her that she wasn't married or that she had her daughters young, everything was an adventure." Agatha smiles. Her eyes twitch, as if they don't really know what to do with her cheeks scrunching towards them. The undertaker thinks that he hasn't seen her smile since her first marriage at nineteen. Teddy steps forward next.

"My sisters were like a little gang. When we were kids they had matching yellow bicycles, and when they would speed towards you with their crazy determined-ness, you were a little scared." Teddy laughs nervously, adjusting his tie. "We knew we were the kids who lived on the edge of town in the house where our dad stuffed dead animals and our mom helped women have babies, kind of like the Addams family, I guess. Strange, but warm. Just the right amount of weird." Teddy looks out at the small crowd. He feels the dozens of eyes on him and feels a chill run down his spine. He doesn't like this kind of attention in the best of times. A flash of red at the back of the room catches his eye. Teddy feels frozen to the spot. A high pitched giggle resounds through the room and he hears footsteps running in a circle behind him. He turns to look but sees nothing, only his sisters motioning for him to keep going.

"I…I don't know what to say, really. It's a tragedy. Not only did we lose our baby sister, we lost our nieces, too. We lost a lot, in that fire. Luna and Lola won't ever get a chance to be the weird kids, or the popular kids, or form a girl gang with yellow bikes. Uhh…that's all I've got."

"Margot was too young to ever try and steal my boyfriends," Sylvia started speaking before she stepped forward to the microphone, "and that's what I loved about her growing up. She was my squishy little sidekick. I'm sorry, that wasn't very kind. I guess where we weren't kind in words, we were kind in other things. I've lost a sister, a really, really great sister. And my daughter's lost her cousins. Three cousins, not two. There really isn't anything else to say. It just… it just sucks."

CHAPTER 8

Agatha is fifteen, sitting on the porch in the snow. She sucks on a cigarette. Her mother sits in the front room dying the grey from her hair. It reminds her of barbed wire spray-painted black. Agatha's lily-shaped lungs feel like they're made of wire. The pond out front is scratched from skating, like a ball of chicken wire. Agatha sucks on a cigarette she stole from her older sister's boyfriend, Nick. She shivers in her father's old plaid jacket.

"Aggy, Aggy, Aggy. Smoking?" Twelve-year old Margot leers at Agatha over crossed arms. The young teenager wears a furry pink sweater, her black bangs cut blunt over her eyes.

"Go away, Marg."

"You know mom's in the front room."

"I can see her. I'll duck if she turns around."

"Is it one of Nick's?"

"What's it to you? Go play with your Barbies."

"Threw them out."

"Whatever. Leave me alone."

"You know mom says you're too skinny and that you're trying to look all Courtney Love to impress Nick."

"Whatever."

"Dad agrees with her."

"Whatever, Margot." Agatha shoves the younger girl and drops the cigarette. "Look what you've done now," she says, reaching to pick it out of the snow, a tiny bullet hole of black ash. The girls hear footsteps and Agatha kicks snow over the butt.

"Hey, guys," Sylvia pops from around the side of the house, "What's up?" Her black hair is short and spiky. Three wire, black-frosted girls on a porch in the snow.

"Agatha! Smoking? I'll tell mom." Sylvia laughs.

"Shame we can't hang your fat lips on the clothesline, Syl." Agatha sneers.

"Agatha, stop it. That's mean." Margot hates seeing her sisters argue.

"Whatever, Agatha. I'm going to town."

"Where's your necklace?" Margot's hand jumps to her bee.

"In my room."

"But we always wear them." Sylvia says.

"I don't always want to look like you two and mom."

"You'll always look like each other," Teddy emerges from the frosted garden, "Mind if I come to town, Syl? I gotta pick up some stuff."

"Sure, Ted. Come on."

Agatha pulls out another cigarette and lights it. Margot swats at it and pretends to choke on the smoke. Teddy smiles at them as he jumps into the passenger seat of the old turquoise truck their parents let them use. Sylvia turns the engine over and air sputters out of the vents. The condensation from her breath and Teddy's whorls, shakes and ruptures in the cab of the truck. They leave the driveway and head down the short road to town. In nicer weather they'd walk. The passenger seat window has been replaced with a garbage bag and the air beats at it.

Teddy points out a snail, crushed on the mat by his foot. "It looks like a small eyeball. You should see it, Syl." She shakes her head.

"You're so weird, Ted. But that's why I love you the best." Teddy tries unsuccessfully to contain his grin. It is so difficult to breach the invisible walls that hold in his sisters. "Shit, looks like mom forgot to take those books back to the library," says Sylvia, straining to look at a pile of soggy books in the jump seat behind her.

"And someone left the windows down again." Teddy means this teasingly but Sylvia hardens. He twists and grabs one of the books, *The Turn of the Screw.*

"Did you ever end up finishing this?" He flashes the cover at Sylvia.

"No," she says, her voice still hard and her chin jutting towards the road in front. "Did you, Mr. Smart Guy?"

Teddy sighs and sticks a Tragically Hip cassette in the tape player. The hum of the guitar matches the rattle of the precariously attached front bumper.

CHAPTER 9

The male honeybee—the drone, exists only to mate with the queen. He is expendable once he provides this service to the colony. Any drones that remain around the hive in the Fall will be driven from the colony before cold weather sets in. Honey stores are too precious to waste on a sperm donor. But Teddy, always the worker bee, has become the propolis—the bee glue—holding his sisters together. Sometimes he tires of their secret, sisterly language, the language he stopped understanding when puberty blazed through their house.

Teddy met Tasia at the Valley Hotel. It was a slow night. A Wednesday. November. Unusually warm. He didn't even have a jacket to throw over his blue plaid shirt. The hotel was across the street from his shop. That week, he was mounting an albino peacock for a local farmer. It was a tedious, time-consuming job and Teddy had a deadline. The creature was to be a Christmas gift for the farmer's wife. The farmer it belonged to began to feed it poison as soon as it had reached adulthood, so that it would die before its feathers were sullied by age. The farmer liked to describe the poisoning, laughing himself backwards over his round belly. He brought treats to the bird. Clucked his tongue at it. Stroked its crown. The bird trusted him.

Teddy sat at the bar. He held the cold glass to his head. A vein near his temple throbbed into the condensation. The trill of the VLTs mingled with a Johnny Cash song. Teddy was accustomed to smaller birds, and had mastered pulling brains out with tweezers and peeling skin using his fingers, but this peacock was enormous, and everything had to be done slowly, and on such a grand scale, and so nothing stained the ivory feathers. He had just finished a twelve-hour shift, and his hands smelled of chemicals.

"Hello, you must be Edward. Heard a lot about you," Teddy shifted so that he was looking through the pale lager at a woman. Well, a blob, really. A blob that he could discern was a woman from her voice, and, he thought, from the way the bottom half of the blob was at a different angle from the top half, which was shimmering. Teddy hadn't said a word to anyone all day. The bartender knew what to bring him. He looked at the blob, and considered its shape. Wavy, like an articulated weasel. The blob spoke again.

"Don't mean to intrude,"

"Oh," Teddy started, removing the glass from his forehead. "Sorry, yes, I'm Teddy Morris,"

"I'm Tasia. I've just moved here, and my new neighbour's kid shot my cat."

"Oh, well, I…I'm sorry. Would you, would you like a drink?" Teddy shifted uncomfortably, aware that his forehead was dripping with condensation from the glass.

"I've got one, actually," Tasia waved her glass at him. "Thanks. I was hoping you could taxidermy Bowie for me. He was a lovely cat."

"Oh…oh yes, of course. The vet must have him still, I'm guessing."

"Yes, wait…did you think I was using my dead cat to try and get you to buy me a drink?" Tasia threw her head back and laughed.

"Oh no, of course not…well, yes actually. I'm sorry. Long day."

"I like to think I'm a little more subtle than that, Mr. Morris," Tasia leans on the counter and sips her drink. "I am new in town, after all. Can't be too forward. People will talk, you know."

Teddy chuckled. "But yes, I can definitely do that for you. I've got a large piece that needs to be finished in two days but I can fit

Bowie in after that."

"Thank you, Edward. I really appreciate that. Can I have the vet drop him off tomorrow?"

"Call me Teddy. Tomorrow's good." Tasia smiles at Teddy and he finds her quite pretty. She has a mess of copper curls and bright green eyes. "You can sit down, you know. I don't need all these chairs to myself." Tasia laughs and hops onto the stool next to him.

Teddy thinks back to this night as Tasia cradles his head in her lap. He is still in his crumpled suit from the funeral.

"It was a lovely service…" Tasia begins. Teddy laughs and snot shoots out of his nose onto her stockings. His eyes are puffy.

"It was a joke, really. Our family's weird enough without painting dead eyes on corpses. I don't know why we did that. Not all traditions…"

"It was in her will, Ted, you had to do it."

"Doesn't really make it any less creepy." Teddy sits up and kisses Tasia. "I'm itching to do something, Tas. I think I might go into work for a bit, try to shake off today."

"No, Teddy. Remember what your dad used to tell you? That you can't work with dead things until you've accepted your own mortality. I don't think that fresh grief and taxidermy mix. Not right now, at least. Let's order a pizza and watch Monty Python. Okay?" Teddy nods. "Your work will be there tomorrow." Tasia gets up and walks over to the fridge. "Heads up!" She tosses a beer at Teddy and cracks one for herself. He grins, then sucks the foam from the top of the can as it fizzes open.

***

It's a Tuesday night and Matthew is on a field trip with his students— band camp or something, Sylvia can't quite remember. Agatha is looking after Ella so Sylvia can have a night to herself— she's the only one who hasn't had a moment of peace since the deaths. She planned on mapping out her climbing trip, but instead finds herself slow and sad.

She lies on the back porch, a pack of Camels at her side, torn open clumsily. She balances a bottle of some Japanese whiskey a friend brought over on her stomach. Her belly is hard and white, framed by black underwear and a Mountain Equipment Co-op shirt cut just under the chest. It is quiet in her neighbourhood. Her porch faces a steep drop into a creek. Her phone buzzes, the vibration interrupting her music, grunge music that makes her nostalgic for puberty.

She ignores it, closes her eyes and waits for the music to resume. The air tickles the three black hairs around her navel, and she fingers the C-section scar beneath. The doorbell rings. With a sigh, Sylvia sits up. She checks her phone, lit up with a text.

It's Jamie. Can I come in?

She can hear Agatha in her head, giving a lecture at the local community centre. *Honeybee sex occurs in mid-air, when the queen flies out in search of mates. Drones compete for the chance to mate with their queen, swarming around her as she flies.*

He says hi casually, as she wraps her forearm around her stomach. She stands in the doorway. Sylvia tells him that she thought he was still living the dirt-bag life down south, in Yosemite.

"You wanted to be a stone monkey, like we'd always planned."

"Yeah," he says, "I am. I wanted to spend a few months in the Rockies, though. Thought I'd stop by, see my old partner." She hesitates and sighs, digging her nails into her collarbone, gripping it like a small hold on a rock wall or a long crack in Squamish.

"Okay, well, come in. I was just on the porch."

"There's no chairs out here, Syl." Jamie says. Sylvia lies down on the blanket and lights a cigarette. She offers him whiskey but he wants beer.

"Don't have any." Sylvia says. Jamie grabs the square bottle and takes a swig.

"Just you tonight?"

"Yep." The two sit in silence on Sylvia's blanket. She offers Jamie the cigarette. He sucks deeply.

"I thought you quit?"

"I had Ella a year ago."

"You look good, are you training again?"

"Since I got home from the hospital."

"Good." Jamie turns to her, his brown eyes big, his face more youthful than most climbers, free of a five o'clock shadow and scars. "Hey, I'm sorry about your sister, Syl."

"I know," Sylvia says as she stands up, her arms wrapped around her thin frame. "What do you want, Jamie? It's not like you to take a break from climbing. I thought we were done when I got pregnant. You said I'd given up and you needed a partner who wouldn't take breaks."

"I just—"

"I'm leaving. Next week. I'm gonna try El Cap again."

"But you have a baby."

"I'm a shit mom."

"Well, probably, but—"

"Why are you here, Jamie?"

"Your sister died and I wanted to make sure you were okay."

"You only ever cared about the rock, not me, not anyone."

Sylvia walks into the house. She sits on the toilet, her shorts around her ankles, and crosses her legs. She tries to pee a little bit to make her departure convincing, but she can't. Sylvia rips off a long chunk of toilet paper and shoves it into her eyes, her face screwed up, her heart racing. She contorts herself, bends over the top of her crossed legs, bouncing deeper into the stretch and biting her knee. Afraid that her breath has become audible, she inhales deep from the back of her throat, and imagines waves crashing against her legs.

She stands up, and faces the mirror. Flushed, her face is splotchy and jagged. She blows her nose into a nest of toilet paper and bites her lip, running cold water over her hands and holding them to her cheeks and chest. She grabs a sweatshirt and tosses it over her pajamas.

Eventually, a brave drone will make his move. As he grasps the queen, the drone everts his penis using a contraction of his abdominal muscles and hemostatic pressure, and inserts it tightly into the queen's reproductive tract. He immediately ejaculates with such explosive force that the tip of his penis ruptures, and is left behind inside the queen.

"Want a coffee, Jamie?" Sylvia yells out onto the porch. She measures enough grounds for two cups.

"Only if it's Fratello," Jamie answers. Sylvia smiles.

"Of course." She turns around, a tin camping cup in her hand. Jamie is standing by the kitchen table.

"Remember the Bugaboos?" Jamie asks, "That summer was great. Great climbs."

"We were a lot younger when we did the Bugs." Sylvia replies.

"We're not even in our thirties, Syl. Come on."

"Have a kid and try to tell me that." Sylvia says. Jamie looks quickly at the ground. He starts to speak but Sylvia interrupts.

"She's obviously not your kid, Jamie. She looks exactly like Matt, and she isn't a brat like your kid would be."

"She could have been mine so easily, though…" Jamie protests, fidgeting with an old envelope on the counter.

"I thought we weren't going to talk about it." Sylvia says, turning to the bubbling coffee maker.

"You always find a way to bring it up."

Sylvia rolls her eyes. She hands Jamie a cup of coffee.

"There's cream in the fridge." She says.

"Sugar?"

"Counter behind you. Blue pot. How are things with Wendy?" Sylvia inhales the thick scent of coffee, and it feels like tiny, painful sparks are jumping around her brain. This is the last bag of coffee that Margot brought from the coffee shop. After work on Tuesdays, Margot would stop by Sylvia's house and they would talk about their children over coffee. Sylvia always felt protective over her youngest sibling, but since Ella was born she found herself needing Margot and her parenting advice more than she needed anyone. With the smell of coffee she heard the high-pitched squeal of the milk steamer and Margot's voice shouting 'good morning' over the sound. She saw Margot's purple lipstick smile through the steam.

"Things are great, actually." Jamie says, "The wedding is next

May. I sent you an invite." Sylvia stares into her coffee.

"I know."

"Do you think you'll come?"

"I don't think so." Sylvia says, walking into the living room and sitting on the couch. Jamie sits on the other end.

They sip their coffees, staring at each other over the brims of their cups.

"Are these the cups we bought in '09?" Jamie asks.

"Yep, the ugly orange you insisted on."

"It matched the van!"

"God, that van!" Sylvia says, laughing at the memory of the camper van they lived in for a summer while climbing.

"You loved it!"

"When there wasn't so much gear that we had to sleep on top of ropes." Sylvia smiled, trying to push that summer from her mind. She and Jamie were never a couple, but on and off they'd tried to be. Living in a van for two months together was the closest they'd ever come to what they both agreed was probably inevitable. But, as usual, by the time October rolled around, Jamie was restless and Sylvia was tired of him and they parted. Sylvia is inexplicably nostalgic for that summer and fall, the excitement of the rock and the van and the man next to her, and the agonizing gaps in speaking when they returned that felt like betrayal. She is nostalgic for the kind of pain that felt like it was reversible. The kind of pain that didn't mean death or birth and hovered somewhere in between.

"So Ella is just under a year?" Jamie clears his throat.

"Yep. Crawling and everything."

"When are you gonna take her into the mountains?"

"We've taken her on a few hikes, mostly with Margot and her girls, but changing a diaper on a trail is tough." Sylvia chews on her cuticles, her leg bouncing. "Why are you here, Jamie?"

"I told you, I was worried about you after what happened."

"And I told you I was fine." Sylvia replies, fixing her eyes on Jamie.

"Are you sure you don't have any beer?"

"Just some that Matt bought. I think you…" Jamie interrupts her.

"Finish your coffee. We're drinking."

"We already were drinking."

"No, we're really not." Sylvia feels restless, twitchy, like her bones will fall through her skin and roll around on the floor like worms.

"What happened last time won't happen again, Syl. It was a stupid mistake."

"I think you should go."

"We won't get so sloppy this time. We won't break into your brother's shop."

"Jamie. You should go." Sylvia says as she stands, "You're not here to check on me. I don't know what you want but I know it's not to make sure I'm okay. Which I am."

Jamie's smile fades and he watches Sylvia's thin legs skip outside onto the porch, and he rubs his eyes, remembering the last time he caught himself staring at her. He follows her onto the porch, where she is lighting a cigarette, her hair hanging dangerously close to the small flame. Sylvia looks at him with a blank face. Agatha is in her head again.

During her one nuptial flight, the queen will mate with a dozen or more partners, leaving a trail of dead drones in her wake. She stores the sperm for use throughout her life.

Sylvia feels Jamie's warmth as his body comes close to hers. "You're not usually like this, Syl. You're usually more open. You usually trust me." As she turns to face Jamie, to tell him once more to go home, she sees a small girl with black hair in a red dress standing at the end of her driveway. The girl looks at Sylvia, and raises a small hand in a gentle wave. Sylvia feels Jamie's breath on her neck but she cannot move, her eyes locked with the girl's. Sylvia gasps when she feels teeth on the back of her neck, whipping around and elbowing Jamie hard in the side as she does so.

"What is WRONG with you?" Sylvia steps backwards, into the balcony. She looks wildly around for the little girl in red. Jamie looks amused. "Get out! I don't want you here." Sylvia is yelling, now, and shaking. She walks towards the steps that lead to the driveway. "You broke my heart, you don't care about anyone. Where does Wendy think you are?" She keeps yelling as she looks for the little girl, looking back at Jamie once in a while. "What are you hoping to get out of this, Jamie? I don't want you here. The funeral was days ago and if you cared you would have been THERE, not showing up on my doorstep to drink my husband's beer and 'reminisce.'"

Jamie is walking close behind Sylvia.

"What are you looking for, Sylvia? What's wrong with you?" Jamie watches as Sylvia disappears around the side of the house. The door to the house next door opens and a dog runs out. It sniffs the ground and barks at Jamie. The owner peeks out, a middle-aged man in sweatpants. He raises his eyebrows at Jamie, who shrugs.

Sylvia is sitting in the damp grass beside her fence, unsure if there was ever a girl, when she hears Jamie's footsteps.

"You know," he says, "we used to get along so well. But now, now you're fucking crazy." Jamie kicks at the grass. Sylvia scoffs. She turns her face from him, worried about the streetlights catching on her tears. She wonders if they ever did really get along.

***

"So, out of our graduating class, who would you fuck first. Tina, Cassie, or Bryanna?" Sylvia shouts, raising her eyebrows at Jamie. The hockey game is at full volume on the small television at the hotel. Jamie leans back and laughs. Sylvia grabs her beer bottle, her wedding ring chimes against the amber glass. It still feels bulky and unfamiliar, a bit like her marriage does.

"Honestly? We're too old for that."

"You asked me this when we were hiking last week!" Sylvia protests, "It's only fair. You can't hide anything from me and you know it."

"Okay, but you asked for it. You, Sylvia Morris, are number one on my would-fuck list."

"It's Sylvia Black, actually." Sylvia rolls her new name off of her tongue slowly. "And, I knew it. After all these years, I knew it."

"Oh shut up," Jamie says, "I've spent literal days of my life belaying you and staring at your ass."

"You say that like I haven't done the same." Sylvia replies.

"Remember that time we got snowed into our tent and we got naked to stay warm?"

"Survival 101. Plus, we agreed it was all about the rock, or the ice, or the mountain."

"Yeah, we had so much self-control back then," Jamie says, eyeing Sylvia's ring.

"More like exhaustion," says Sylvia, looking Jamie in the eyes. "After 14 hours of climbing who had the energy?" The waitress that comes to their table is short and plump, sort of like a young grandma the way her hair is permed, thinks Sylvia. She can hear the VLTs behind her, the die-hards holding their glass of Coors to their mouths with one hand and pulling on the lever with the other. Men in jerseys yell at the television. She feels her sit bones sink into the wooden chair. She remembers her sister's advice from years ago. If you want to seduce someone, ask for a drag of their cigarette.

"Got any cigarettes?" she asks, then adds with a wiggle of her eyebrows, "Babe?" Jamie smirks.

"Yeah, let's go." They leave their beers on the table and head past a group of older men. The room spins, and Sylvia finds herself gripping Jamie's arm. He places his hand over hers. Their hands grate on each other, sandpaper on an emery board. Sylvia bites her lip, tasting waxen red lipstick.

Outside, Jamie lights a cigarette, and passes it to Sylvia after a drag.

"So, babe, huh? I forgot about that." He says, smiling as Sylvia inhales long and hard. She exhales into his face and laughs.

"I did too, until now."

"We were such dorks in high school." Jamie shakes his head. "Fourteen and calling each other babe."

"I mean," replies Sylvia, "that's probably why we didn't have much luck dating other people."

Jamie takes the cigarette back from Sylvia and they stare at each other under a street light until the cigarette is burnt out. It's a Tuesday and the hockey game is nearly over. The bar is closing soon, so they order another round and they sit by the fire, inching closer and closer to one another. Jamie's lips are chapped and Sylvia's lipstick fades, ten glasses now bearing its mark. Jamie cups Sylvia's left breast through her black tank top, wagging his eyebrows at her, thumbing her nipple until it is hard. She giggles, and they lock eyes in a staring contest.

"Remember that game we used to play in junior high?" Jamie asks.

"Which one? Truth or dare?"

"No, 'are you nervous yet'."

"Oh, god," Sylvia says, "Yeah, I remember."

"We'd be better at it now."

"Oh, come on, Jamie. It's such a stupid game, you touch someone until they get nervous and make you stop."

"Or you both get detention." Jamie reaches under Sylvia's shirt and pinches her nipple, hard. "Are you nervous yet?"

"No." He places his hand higher on her chest. Her heart beats hard into his hand.

"Liar."

"Jamie—"

He leans over the table and bites her lip, eyes wide open. He pulls on it as he moves backwards.

"What the hell, Jamie?! That hurt!"

"Wanna dance?"

"There's no music in here."

"Jukebox. I'll pick the first song," Jamie pulls out a loonie. "You're gonna love this."

Sylvia stares at her hands as he walks to the jukebox by the pool tables. The dead white skin on her palms curls around the raw pink bubbles of blisters, like the film that forms on soup left out overnight. *I Miss You* by Blink 182 starts playing.

"Really, Jamie?"

"What? I was in your creative writing class when you wrote poems about Travis Barker, remember?" Jamie grabs Sylvia's hand and her breath jumps out of her. "Plus, we can slow dance to this one."

"Ugh, Jamie… This is so embarrassing. What if people see?"

"Syl, there's like one other person in here now."

"You're drunk."

"You're drunk." Jamie pulls Sylvia into his chest.

"I am a little drunk," she agrees, leaning her head on his shoulder.

"No shit, babe."

"Here we go again."

"It's like we're sixteen again." He teases, brushing his lips on the top of her head.

"Let's not revisit our teenaged years, please." Sylvia buries her face in Jamie's neck, sighs, and then bites him, hard. He yelps and Sylvia laughs.

"Revenge! Give me some of your beer." Jamie holds his glass up to her lips, sloshing beer down her shirt.

"I'll get it for you," he dips his head, sticking his tongue onto her breastbone, "there you go, all clean. Let's get out of here."

"And go where?" Sylvia asks, thinking of the coolness of air brushing against her chest where Jamie licked her. This feels right, she thinks. Jamie just needed some incentive to finally admit that he loved her back. Something to help him get over what Sylvia assumed was shyness. Something like a marriage to another man.

Sylvia sighs, "I have keys to Teddy's shop."

"Perfect. I'll go pay. Grab our coats."

There are few sights more unsettling during sex than a rabbit cut in half and stuffed, waiting for the two halves to be sewn back together. The rabbit keen and poised, its torso stuffed with plastic. Its hind legs and buttocks resting a few inches away. Sylvia stares at this animal as Jamie moves behind her, locking her eyes with its glass ones. The rabbit whispers to her that no, this doesn't feel so right after all.

Sylvia stands in the shower the next morning, her head pounding and her fingers running up and down her spine, bruised from the linoleum floor. A scab is forming just below her bra line where

Jamie thrust against her, burning the floor into her skin. Matthew comes into the shower, his eyes red with exhaustion from taking his students into the mountains.

"Hey, love." He kisses her and closes his eyes to the hot water. Sylvia wraps herself around her husband, feeling his soft flesh worm between her fingers where Jamie's hard body had refused to sink.

When Jamie said that he didn't think people were meant to only fuck the same person until they died, she heard him say that people weren't meant to love just one person until they died. So she found her spine digging into the linoleum floor of her brother's taxidermy shop while Jamie ground on top of her while her husband graded ninth grade laboratory reports in a tent and listened to twelve year-olds snore.

In her memory she watched her and Jamie from above. Her face was blank and she was drunk and in that moment she knew that Jamie would never love her back.

***

Sylvia leans against the railing of her porch, keeping a lookout for the little girl. She can hear Jamie's anger echo in the night. The shrillness of his tires on the hot summer pavement, the sting of his words. She sighs, knowing that like a flood this was inevitable and that it would happen again and again and all that would remain would be bruises and teeth and a half drunk beers where there shouldn't be. This is always how it is with Jamie—a hurricane, a flood, a natural disaster. A mess, but never a mess as cruel as tonight. She has to cut him out. She can climb on her own.

Sylvia wanders into her daughter's bedroom, and picks up the rabbit that Teddy gave her as a present. Fur as soft and white as a stuffed toy, the nails and teeth removed. She hugs it to her chest and cries.

CHAPTER 10

Lulu Morris kneads bread, knuckle over knuckle. Her hands crack open raw over the kitchen sink. Steel wool gags the drain. Her shadow is long in the dusky kitchen. Her hair falls like Spanish moss, knotted and the black giving way to grey.

Her husband, Casper has just given their four children some bad news. He takes the stiff body of the family cat into his shed, a new challenge; a chance to immortalize their childhood with borax and stuffing.

Sylvia's lips bounce off of Margot's dough head. Margot cries. Silas was twelve years old. Her small hands tangle in the mud-caked tresses of her dentist Barbie. The girls sit on the porch, holding each other as the sun goes down, rocking from the news.

They look on as Agatha tends the plants in the front garden. She wakes them up, leaves between fingers, humming in the dark with crust in her eyes. The first glimmers of frost settle on the wheat-coloured grass, and the snails go to sleep under the thin ice.

Autumn startles them and the garden dries up. Lulu and Casper run from the frost, leaving their children to catch the yellow school bus under the lazy eye of the neighbour while they drive north to spend a few days in West Edmonton Mall, soaking up fabricated sunlight, sleeping in a tiki-themed room, and attending a small taxidermy conference. They could have taken the children, sure, but they never have time to themselves these days.

Old Ms. Heck doesn't check on the children the first evening without their parents, or the second. They stay up watching *The Twilight Zone* and eating instant mashed potatoes. Sylvia assures her siblings that Ms. Heck will be there in the morning to usher them to school. They stay up until well past midnight, and the next morning Teddy wakes up first, his littlest sister's toes in his eyes.

"We forgot to bring the tomatoes in last night," Sylvia wakes with a start, sprawled on the living room floor swathed in old crocheted blankets.

"I don't like bringing them in," replies Agatha. "I have to walk on the organ-y grass."

"Suck it up, Aggie. It's just the bits from last year, they're all decomposed now."

When Lulu and Casper return, they are speech and speechless in umber October, plucking leaves from their children's hair, kissing dirt from their chins. Lulu's cracked hands caress Casper's grey face. Teddy looks on with violet moon eyes, the cold winter gone from his parents' eyes. Margot hiccoughs from her bed, asleep and dreaming of burnt August and locusts.

CHAPTER 11

Agatha is determined not to lose her hives this winter. She's already lost so much. She sews black tarps together to make covers for the hives.

This time last year, she was barreling down Deerfoot Trail to a ballet recital, trying to save a marriage she didn't really care about anymore. Drew's daughter was in an amateur production of Swan Lake. Agatha felt, in that car, in the snow, with the heat turned all the way up, that she was a bee being overwintered. The snow cocooned her car. Her jacket and scarf and sweater and mitts cocooned her. Agatha puffed on cigarettes with the windows rolled up, ashing onto her parka. When an ember blew onto her neck, the burn stinging her, she decided to roll down the windows and not walk into the recital smelling like an ashtray. Her phone rang. It went to voicemail. "Where are you? The show's already started. Danielle will be so upset if you miss another one of her shows. She worked so hard. You saw her practice. Please, just hurry. Just show up." Agatha drove faster. She was only ten minutes away. Her bag held three negative pregnancy tests and a stuffed ballerina mouse.

Agatha is determined to not lose her hive this year. She needs a healthy brood. She needs something to thrive, something to live.

The auditorium door creaked open loudly as Agatha tried to locate Drew and his ex-wife and all of the grandparents in one of the rows. Heads whipped around at the noise and Agatha felt as though she was staring into a mass of beetles, their angry eyes glimmering at her. On stage, ten year-olds in garish makeup twirled and stumbled. She texted Drew. He stood and beckoned her over. She tripped over an older woman's cane and nearly ended up in her father-in-law's lap. Her bag fell onto the floor. And she hurriedly snatched it up. Drew shifted seats so she could sit next to him. He squeezed her knee with his hand but didn't look at her, his nostrils flared towards the stage. Agatha wondered how Margot sat through so many school plays and dance recitals and for a moment she felt alright about the negative pregnancy tests.

Agatha sews with a fervour. It has already snowed. It is September. She can't lose the bees.

A small blonde girl with her face painted gaunt and hair pulled back tight stood on top of a scaffolding. Below her was a large gym mat. The music built. The girl, who seemed impossibly small and impossibly high in the air, crashed to the mat. Agatha gasped. The audience erupted in applause.

These bees cost money. These bees are still new to their environment. These bees are her children, her brood.

Danielle ran into Drew's arms, and Agatha fumbled to grab the bouquets of roses he'd been holding so he could pick up his daughter and spin her around. The little girl smiled at Agatha.

"Aggie! You came! Did you see me die? I was so scared of the height at first but I DID it!" Agatha nodded and tucked a hair behind Danielle's cheek.

"You were perfect, absolutely perfect, Dani."

Danielle's mom, Mary, swept the child out of Drew's arms. "Should we celebrate with ice cream, sweetie?" she asked. Danielle nodded, her eyes gleaming.

"Can Daddy and Aggie come, Mama?"

"Of course they can."

Agatha cannot lose these bees. She finishes the first cover.

Drew didn't have any siblings. Neither did Danielle. Agatha

longed to have Margot's hand to squeeze as she sat in a Dairy Queen with her in-laws and her husband's ex-wife's family. Danielle sat between Drew and her mom. Agatha sat across from them, between both grandfathers.

Drew and Mary talked quietly over Danielle's head as she happily slurped up a chocolate sundae. Both grandfathers had hamburgers. Both grandmothers sipped on small cups of ice water. Mary occasionally had a bit of sundae with her own spoon. A melting banana split sat in front of Drew. Outside it snowed. In Agatha's bag were three negative pregnancy tests. She'd given Danielle the stuffed mouse.

It starts to snow as Agatha shimmies the covers over the hives. Not this year, she thinks. This year will be a fertile one.

It is 11:30pm in the Valley, and Agatha stands alone in the middle of the four-way-stop. The stop signs are at least four times the size of those in the city. Though it is August the wind blows cold, sending snowflakes in circles around her. The streetlights illuminate her; a gaping black woman-shape standing in the street, arms out, wearing a silk slip and nothing else. Her hair is piled on her head and the points of her shoulders grip the straps of her slip like the nobs on dress hangers. On Monday nights, no one stands outside of the hotel. The only people stirring in the town are in the distance, background noise. The one-armed-man lopes alongside his friend who drives a John Deer lawn tractor down one of the side streets, headed to the gas station for smokes.

"That's the old midwife's daughter, ain't it?" The one-armed-man, Joseph, leers at the pale figure in the street.

"What the hell's she doin'? It's cold as balls," the man on the lawn tractor says. The men shake their heads at the young women floating in the middle of the four-way stop."

"Always thought she looked like a nutter,"

"Bit of a slut, too, if you ask me."

"Hate this snow. It's August for fuck-sake."

"Her dad still a taxidermist?"

"Dead, but maybe the son can stuff you a new arm. Just steal one from the funeral home."

"Heard he does some freaky shit with animals."

"What's that one do?"

"Fuck if I know, stands in the middle of the fuckin' road."

"Probably still fucked up after her sister getting killed."

"Right, forgot about that."

"Snorky, it's freezing. Let's get those smokes and get outta here."

Snorky kills the gas on the tractor and swings his leg over the machine to dismount. His back is arched like a cat and his arms hang down to his knees. He wears a threadbare Guns n' Roses shirt and faded Levi's. His hooked nose sticks out past the earflaps of his Budweiser hat.

The Valley isn't really a valley. It is two small towns connected by a winding road nestled just below the Rocky Mountains. The road follows a river, or rather, a riverbed. Flooding wiped out the structure of the river, so that a shallow, angry beast is all that remains. In the summer of 2005, Agatha, Margot, and Sylvia snuck out of the house late at night with a bottle of their mother's gin. Sylvia hid it under her housecoat. The three girls wore fluffy purple robes with nothing underneath. They reached the river and threw off their robes, b-lining for three large rocks in the middle of the river. They lay like mermaids on the rocks, the air tickling their breasts. They giggled, balancing on the rocks on one foot, leaping onto the middle one and clinging to each other. Three water spirits, white and wispy in the dark. The moon bounced off of their skin and the bottle as they passed it back and forth.

CHAPTER 12

The trend towards celebrity-inspired taxidermy pleased Teddy. His teenage years were spent turning rodents into rock stars. A shelf in his bedroom held his favourite musicians: Beaver Bowie, Boy George Marmot, Robert Smith Porcupine, Ian Curtis Chipmunk, Morrissey Mouse, Joan Jett Woodchuck, Stevie Nicks Rat.

In the early morning, Teddy blinks the sleep out of his eyes. Tasia sleeps next to him, snoring loudly, her thick curls sticking straight up. She is cocooned into an old patchwork quilt. He runs a soft hand over her figure and sighs, looking at his surroundings, thinking about the day before, the funeral.

Agatha bangs on her brother's door for three minutes before she lets herself into his house, a repurposed rail car in a circle of trees and swamp. The once metallic colour has been painted a forest green with a gaudy mural of boulders, like an attempt at camouflage. The house is exceedingly tidy. His white noise machine whirs from the bedroom. Agatha fills a mug with water from the rain barrel and pours it into a kettle. She can hear Tasia snoring.

Agatha turns the stove on and the sour smell of gas fills the room. A mobile hangs above the kitchen sink, branches twisted into a lopsided circle with mice dressed as characters from *A Midsummer Night's Dream* dangling from fishing line. Margot's favourite story as a child. It is the mobile Teddy made for the baby shower years ago, for her first born.

"Teddy, get up! We have to meet with the lawyers today." A grunt comes from the bedroom and Agatha fills the kettle with water, placing it on the stove. Her husband hadn't come to the funeral. He was off with his new girlfriend in Turks and Caicos. Typical. Agatha stares at the mobile above the sink, listening to the hot water rumble in the kettle. The kettle screams, like her screams as she pushed the dead child out of her body those years ago.

Agatha pours the hot water over rough-ground coffee in a French press. Tasia wanders into the kitchen. "Hey Aggie," she pecks Agatha on the cheek, "how are you doing?"

"I'm alright, just so much legal stuff to do, you know. Coffee?"

"Yes, please," replies Tasia. "Teddy's just getting dressed. You look great."

"Oh, thanks," Agatha pats the front of her dress, a black shift.

"How are the bees?"

"Oh," Agatha smiles. "They're great. Just replaced the old queen. I think I'm going to get a lot of honey this year."

"When do you want me to come over to help make the candles?"

"Probably not till the end of the month, I don't think they'll be ready until then. How are the animals?" Agatha asks.

"Rabbits are almost ready to go to slaughter, and I butchered some chickens last night if you want some meat. Teddy wants to stuff some of the rabbits but I think we should just use the fur." Teddy comes out of his room, dressed in black pants and a red sweater. He kisses Tasia on the lips and Agatha on the forehead.

"I heard Jamie's back in town." Teddy says. Agatha passes him a mug of coffee.

"Yeah. Does Syl know?"

"Don't think so."

"I'm supposed to look after Ella tomorrow night while Matt's away. Maybe I should cancel so Syl doesn't do something she regrets."

"She's a grown up, Agatha."

"I know, but Matt…"

"Just leave it. It's not our business," Teddy says.

"She's our sister." Agatha glares at him. "We only have one of those left, remember?"

Tasia pipes up, "I'll grab a chicken from the freezer for you, Aggie. Just make sure you bring me the bones afterwards, okay?"

"Sure, Tasia," Agatha says, distracted by her staring contest with Teddy. Tasia disappears into another room.

"Teddy, I think Syl is planning on leaving."

"Why? Did she say anything? What about Ella?"

"Teddy, she's blaming herself, or something. She said she just has to go and try some route again."

"With Jamie?"

"No, solo." Agatha leans back on the counter. "You know, she might be the oldest but she worries me the most. She worried mom, too." Teddy nods.

"Does Matt know?" he asks.

"I don't think so."

***

The bumblebee queen digs herself a hole, a clay pot in the ground. She waits in stillness, breathings slow and docile as her colony sleeps or dies. In the spring she builds a honey pot, a waxen kiln in which to lay eggs and rest like a hen.

The honeybee queen does not sleep through the overwinter. She is alive and fertile, the hive buzzing and beating against the frost.

***

"Thank you for coming today. August long weekend is just around the corner and we are apparently supposed to have an early winter this year." Agatha looks tired, spent. Her dark eyebrows, overgrown reaching towards each other. Her pale skin is pockmarked and blotchy, "I would like to use this opportunity to formally resign as the head of the committee. If there is nobody willing to take on this role, then the Bee Meetings will conclude after a wonderful four years."

The rest of the people on the committee shift uneasily in their seats, their eyes fixed on the black liquid in their mugs.

"It's been a rough month for my family, and I'm sure you'll forgive us for being less involved while we process the death of our sister and nieces."

Agatha nods at Teddy.

"Yes. Sylvia has left for California, as you know, and I will be shutting down the shop for a week. Agatha is going to take some time as well."

Tasia pipes in, "I'm taking a short leave from the hospital to spend time with Ted and Aggie. The investigation has taken a toll on all of us."

"My bees," Agatha spits out a sob, "they have all died or gone." Her bony hands clutch her mug, and she hunches over it, her long black hair dragging in her coffee.

***

The new queen did not survive. In cases of Colony Collapse disorder, most or all of the worker bees will disappear, leaving behind the queen, some nurse bees, and any immature bees. A week after Margot's funeral, Agatha's colony collapses, and the new queen bee dies.

***

Jamie is sitting at a table by the window of Wayward Coffee Co. when Sylvia sits down across from him, Ella in her arms.

"Sylvia, how are you?" Jamie smiles and gestures to Ella sucking on a yellow pacifier. "This must be Emma!"

"Her name is Ella."

"You look great, better, better than I expected. You were a bit unhinged last time I saw you."

Sylvia glares at him. Ella's eyes are wide, darting around the room. She struggles in Sylvia's arms to reach Jamie's bright blue coffee cup. Sylvia places a pack of cigarettes on the table, holding Ella in one arm and fiddling with the cigarettes with her free hand. She takes one out and puts it back, then another. Almost like she is playing some kind of instrument. She sucks in her cheeks.

"I—I miss you, Syl. I really do. Well, the old you. I hope you're doing okay."

"I'm fine, Jamie." Sylvia sighs, "How are you? How is Wendy?"

"Oh, you know."

"Do I?" Sylvia cocks an eyebrow. Ella grabs a cigarette and Sylvia gently tugs it from her hand, putting the pack back in her pocket. She kisses Ella's forehead and Ella grabs a handful of the hair that's fallen out of her bun.

"I guess you wouldn't know." Jamie stares at his coffee, his mouth twitching. "The wedding's off. I ended it about a week ago."

"Of course you did. This is broken engagement what, number three?"

"It's not like that, Syl,"

"Yeah, it is, Jamie. You get scared that you'll finally be fucking happy and then you leave."

"It's just never felt—" Jamie starts to speak but Sylvia interrupts, bouncing Ella on her knee.

"And every time you decide to start over or get confused, you drag me into it and you show up and you play with my head and I'm sick of it. I'm not your fucking plan B, Jamie." Jamie's forehead crinkles.

"You never were my plan B, Sylvia,"

"Your plan C, then. Whatever, it's all the same,"

"You weren't my plan C, either, Syl."

"What do you want, Jamie? I agreed to meet you only because you had something to tell me."

"I talked to Jordan."

"Great. Your asshole brother that fucked over my dead sister."

"He wanted me to tell you he's sorry about Margot."

"I don't care what he has to say. My brother and sister don't care what he has to say. He's a deadbeat and if he thinks he has any right…"

"Look, Sylvia," Jamie raises his voice, "I know you're pissed, but can you listen to me for just a minute?" Ella begins to cry. Sylvia stares at him.

"Fine, but I need to get Ella out of here. It's too loud for her."

The pair stands on the grass in front of the coffee shop. Sylvia is on her knees, hovering above Ella who crawls in the grass. Jamie's hands are in his pockets, his shoulders hunched. Jamie is tall, a foot or so above Sylvia. She stands up and runs her hand through her hair self-consciously. They stand in silence. Sylvia glances at the coffee shop window. Their reflection is strange, like a funhouse mirror she thinks. Her limbs are too long for her body, her torso is too flimsy for the length of her limbs. Jamie is a large black coat and little else.

"Jordan said he saw Margot that night, the night she died." Jamie says. Sylvia freezes.

"What? Where?" Sylvia asks, swooping down to gather Ella into her arms. She holds her daughter close to her.

"She went over to his place,"

"Why? What did she say? Were the kids with her?"

"I don't know…we don't talk much."

"Why are you telling me this if you don't even have the facts straight, Jamie?" Sylvia's voice is shrill and her grip on Ella tightens. Ella cries, waving her small fists.

"I thought you should know. I don't think Jordan told the RCMP."

"What are you saying, Jamie?" Tears stream down Sylvia's face. Ella cries, and Sylvia holds onto her like she is the only thing she has left.

"I…I don't know, Sylvia. I thought it would help."

"Nothing you do helps me, Jamie. Nothing."

CHAPTER 13

Agatha tried and tried and tried, but it was never enough. She knew she would never have children, by now, but still held out hope. She was first married at nineteen, but after six months of trying, the boy from the supermarket deli left her. She married over and over, slipping her slim figure into the same white dress numerous times, because it always fit. She lost the weight just as she lost the babies.

Every pregnancy, even the phantom ones, felt like an invasion, always marked by shivering. She felt like an old woman at nineteen. She read old wives' tales about pregnancy and fertility. Textbooks from the 1700s. She became superstitious.

The white worm burrowed in the salt, claimed the child for its own.

"I forgot to take a shower," she said to her second husband, at twenty-one, her belly round and quiet, "Would you like to join me?"

She asked her second husband to bind together two branches and place it on her naked belly while they stood under the water.

For years, Agatha was climbing into the tub, over and over. To wash away the blood of menstruation, or miscarriage, or stillborn afterbirth. She tried to escape, went to Europe at twenty-three and in the Parisian hospitals she used to ask a priest to bless mixtures of water and sugar over her taut stomach. Her third husband infused fresh cows' milk with rosemary, and dribbled it onto her rounding belly with his lips.

The third husband wanted to stay, but everything became glass and she tired of him weeping for her. In her third pregnancy with husband number three, she began to forget things.

"Darling, did you put those flowers on my pillow?" the third husband asked. Agatha shook her head and handed him the bar of soap. He bent to wash the toes she could no longer reach, his ankles cracked and echoed.

"Do not force the appetite," the doctor advised, "not all pregnant women have strange cravings."

But everything rotted away. She became convinced a strip of whale bone had lodged itself in her ankle after a trip to Vancouver.

"A pregnant woman should always bathe in the ocean."

Husband number three wondered if this was true, and carried his weak wife to the edge of the sea, cupped foam in his hands and brought it to her belly. The babies kicked, humming from their cage. Words grow scarce in the surf and Agatha clutched her husband's hip bone.

Then, the fever dreams began. She found butterflies and her dead mother's molar underneath her pillow. The week after the daisies appeared where her husband lay his head there were two identical scarlet fish in the kitchen sink when he went to rinse the fresh basil for her tea. They were bright like fresh blood. She couldn't tell if she was dreaming, but she heard her husband whisper, "I have just come back from the ghost town," when he crawled in bed beside her.

Agatha's third husband, Drew, was the mayor of the Valley, and he was scared for his wife. He went to the hotel for a drink when she was in her third trimester with the twins. An old man squinted at him. His hand tightened around his drink.

"When I was young, I used to stare. My wife was so beautiful, like an oil spill, dark and slippery." The man regaled the mayor with his life story and the mayor sipped at his drink, thinking of Agatha.

The bed was too narrow, anyway and with the beacons hidden twitching behind her navel, the third husband developed this habit of sharpening knives, of keeping his eyes open at night, glued to the belly. Her stomach like a bleached jawbone protruded, even maternity clothes couldn't contain the moon of her body. When the babies came into the world still, Agatha simply turned on her side, away from her third husband.

A slow, grey sludge ran down his cheek. It was winter and all the leaves were off the trees when he wheeled her out of the hospital in a wheel-chair. Armed with maxi pads, a lone bee landed on her ring finger, her hands folded in her lap. She wept without moving a muscle in her face and he knew that alongside five babies, he'd also lost his wife.

She stayed for nine more months, until garter snakes flitted under the porch light like a swarm. One morning he found Agatha sitting in bed clutching a locket made of brass and a note written on the back of a receipt for aubergines:

"The spirits of murdered infants crawl through windows and cause mothers to miscarry."

There was no wind that night but the pages of Agatha's books on holistic pregnancy and infertility seemed to vibrate with that sentence. He thought of the first child, the baby that came like a vendor of smoke, the size and weight of a hen's egg.

When Agatha packed her things in the middle of the night to retreat to her mother's old house, her body had tried and failed to give eight children life. Around miscarriage number two she studied under her mother to become a midwife, hoping that some kind of karma would give her a healthy child. She took on the practice once her mother died of cancer, and stayed pregnant for nearly five years, only carrying three children to term. Three children that were born silent, anyway.

Her patients were somehow not frightened by the midwife whose body rejected motherhood, somewhere they had heard that it was good luck. Agatha didn't feel like a good luck charm, however, and a year before Margot's death, and after two hundred successful deliveries, she decided to rear queens more fertile than her. Like a tent she had an open slit and she was sick of men trying to build lamps inside her. If a lamp was to be built, no one could see the naked wick.

***

Agatha drinks half a bottle of wine in the bath every night. She fills the square tub with oils, salts, and flower petals. She smears snail slime and sheep placenta all over her face. It promises to keep her young. She tries to read but she can't get past the first page of any book. A stack of discarded novels lie in a wire basket by the toilet, slowly soaking up moisture and expanding in the damp room. She runs the bath so hot that it scalds her and she cannot feel anything but prickles of heat all over her body. She breathes lemongrass and lavender deeply, closing her eyes so tight that the goop on her face weighs down her lashes. Sometimes when her muscles ache from carrying her dead babies on her hips, she douses the surface of the water with peppermint oil, watching the honey droplets flatten across the water before she slips in, her epidermis writhing with fire and ice, the sensation cutting into her labia, her entire body burning. When the water cools, she drains the tub, sinks to the bottom of the basin, sticks her toes into the drain and feels the water tickle its way along her bones. She watches the tide recede from her pale contours until she lies shivering in an empty tub.

Agatha stands, and blood rushes into her eyes. Naked in the bathtub, white foam from dollar-store bubble-bath slinks down her stomach and disappears between her thighs. She dries her hair and pulls on a pair of black leggings. It is 11 p.m. and Agatha is drunk. She laces up her running shoes and heads out the door. The lights are soft and her eyes are soft and her limbs are soft and all that she feels is softness. She is a pile of feathers running through the streets. The air bites her skin, leaving it blotchy and raw. Her lips shrivel in the cold, dry air. The nights are dark now and her garden is quiet under layers of frost.

A high of minus 17 overnight, the news said. Minus twenty-five with the wind chill. Three blocks from her home she realizes she has forgotten her headphones, and the wind slipping into her ears unnerves her. She jogs on, slapping her feet hard into the packed snow and ice so that she does not slip.

It has been four months since Margot died. Three months and three weeks since the bees. Agatha finds herself staring at the High Country Lodge Senior's home, her head spinning with wine, her lungs straining with cold, her nose leaking.

Once all of the children finished high school and Lulu Morris died in an accident, Casper Morris lived in the senior's home for all of two weeks before he died out of defiance, more than anything. Sixty-eight, fit and nimble, with a failing liver. Agatha recalls her father fondly, staring up at the large retirement facility that he hated. She bends over and spits into the ice, wiping her nose on her sleeve. She kicks at some stray gravel, her stomach heavy and empty, as though the walls are made of thick fabric, the kind that ugly curtains are made of.

Until about fifteen years ago, the lot that Agatha stands on was home to a curious building. At that time it was nearly outside of the town, a looming green barn the size of a football field. The Bargain Barn, it was called, though Agatha didn't know if that was its true name. It might not have had a name. The barn was like a maze to Agatha and her siblings, a dimly lit, musty building with a glass desk at the front. The building at once had no rooms and many rooms. Sometimes it was impossible to wade through to one side without losing her mother. There was a crawlspace in the back book room, where pillows lined the floor. She would crawl into it to read whatever Nancy Drew books she could find. There was a stairway leading to a loft that held sports equipment, where she would sometimes find her father searching for hockey skates as Teddy outgrew his.

Her siblings mostly crawled underneath racks of clothing, jumping out at their mother, playing tag and hide and seek, or wreaking havoc on the toys section, where they would rip open bags of action figures and Barbies, searching for additions to their collections. Time had blurred her memories of the strange building. Sometimes she would remember large brass gateways propped against the barn's interior, other times she would remember stray cats burrowing in forgotten corners. The dirty glass cabinets always held magnificent jewels.

The people that worked in the Bargain Barn didn't seem to mind that children used it as a playhouse, a reading room, or a giant costume trunk. They polished antiques and stowed them away for themselves, neglecting the sweeping in favour of rummaging through donations for a piece of designer underwear.

On Tuesdays, you could buy an entire bag of books for $1.00, and Agatha would often come home to her bedspread covered in novels from her mother. Sundays, a bag of clothes cost $5.00. Whatever you could fit into a Safeway bag was yours for the taking. The children's closets overflowed with whatever their mother lugged home from the Barn. Casper scanned the aisles for fabrics to make clothes for his creations, anything resembling a plaque to mount heads onto, and marbles for strange eyes. Sylvia found her first climbing harness in the Bargain Barn, Margot her first Baby-Alive doll, and Agatha her first midwifery textbook.

As she stands half-drunk and heaving spit onto the ground, Agatha sees the ghost of the Bargain Barn sitting on top of High Country Lodge. The exoskeleton of the green barn squeezes the Lodge, spinning and spinning. The stars spin with it, and the snow warms under Agatha's feet. She walks toward the Barn, a desire to fill the gaps in her memory overwhelming her.

She reaches the door of the Barn, and pries it open. A cloud of dust greets her, settles into her eyebrows. Chalk, moss, sweat, must. She fumbles around for a light-switch but cannot find one. Something is tugging at her leggings. A giggle erupts, and as Agatha turns to see a flash of red dart into the blackness, she trips, her shoelaces knotted together. She pulls out her mobile phone, trying to see the knot well enough to untie it. Small footsteps dart back and forth in the building, the metallic whirring of clothes shoved down a metal rack swirls around her. She shines the feeble light from her cell phone out, catching swarms of dust and little else. Something taps her on the shoulder and she whips around. A giggle. Agatha struggles to stand, her ankle throbbing. She breathes an inquiry into the darkness. Another giggle. More footsteps. More metallic scraping. She tries again to see with the glow of her screen. Again, she catches dust. And then a face. A smiling, round face, with crudely-cut black bangs, freckles like smudges from a permanent marker. She chokes on her breath. The young girl giggles and disappears. An industrial clank sounds and the lights buzz to life. The round metal racks of clothes spin wildly, battery-operated toy cars whir around, running underfoot, a huge beehive descends from the ceiling, the pages of books stuck to it with wax. The little girl giggles, pokes Agatha in the stomach, and runs up a set of stairs. Agatha limps towards the stairs but the girl is already at the top. She reaches towards the bee-hive from the loft, suddenly teetering on roller-skates. Agatha tries to protest, to tell her to back away from the edge, but the small, dark-haired girl slips off of the platform, falling onto the floor littered with toys. Before Agatha can reach her, the bees descend from the hive, covering the girl's struggling body until she is still.

***

"How did you hurt your ankle again?" Teddy sits at the kitchen table, half-amused, while Agatha hops around with one crutch.

"I went running." Agatha tells him.

"At night? In the cold?"

"Well, yes."

"Why would you want to do that?"

"I just felt like it, okay? I felt all restless and spastic so I thought a run might help."

"And you slipped on the ice, of course, because it's winter and you were ill-prepared."

"Yes, Teddy."

"Classic Aggie. For a smart girl you're so dumb sometimes." Teddy eagerly sipped at a mug that Agatha put in front of him.

"How's the shop?"

"It's surprisingly good, actually. Turns out it is trendy to stuff your dead pets. Who would've thought? And I guess natural his-

tory or freak shows or something must be making a comeback because I can't make weird taxidermy fast enough. Did you know a rat
dressed as Donald Trump went for three grand on Etsy last week?
What a time to be alive, Ag," Teddy laughs, swinging his feet onto
the table. "Dad would have got a fucking kick out of this, wouldn't
he?"

Agatha nods in agreement, "I'm going to go back to work, Ted."

"Oh yeah? Indoor bees?"

"No. Work-work. At the hospital."

"Shit, really? Are you ready?"

"Not much use sitting around in perpetual mourning. The hospital says I can start with one shift a week and work my way up to
part-time."

"I'll make sure Tasia keeps an eye out for you." Teddy looks uneasily at his sister.

"She's in a completely different wing, Ted. But thank you."

"Hey, Ag?" Teddy says. Agatha nods, flipping through an issue
of Midwifery Monthly, "I'm starting to think we'll never find out
what happened to Margot."

"I accepted that a long time ago. You should, too."

CHAPTER 14

Bees and wasps evolved from a common ancestor. Istria, the home where the Morris children grew up, was once a haven for a wasp-ish woman, a tortured woman. Casper and Lulu tried to keep their children from learning the reason that their luxurious home was affordable to a taxidermist and a midwife. They sent them to school two towns over. They cultivated a private library to dissuade the children from snooping. They kept away from town meetings and gatherings, and never let the children talk to strangers. Of course, this only lasted for so long, and the four little bees of Istria met the wasp.

Poor Margot was only nine when a well-meaning neighbour invited the children in for tea and regaled them with the history of their home.

"One Tuesday evening in July, seventeen years ago, like this one, actually, muggy and strange, the Wasp– her real name was Giulietta Vespa, which means young wasp—wandered into town and seduced an old man, Mr. Dobbs."

"What does *seduced* mean?" Margot was inquisitive, but not the brightest child.

"Never mind that. Now, Ms. Vespa moved here from Trail, BC—lots of Italians, there—and nobody really knew why. Kept to herself, mostly. She had a very hairy upper lip, and some said her neck was thick with hair too, which is why she wore so many turtlenecks. Anyway, one day she went into town and sat down across from Mr. Dobbs at the Coyote Moon restaurant."

"The one that sells ice cream?" Teddy asks.

"Yes, Edward, the very same. Old Mr. Dobbs wasn't a small man. And he wasn't actually very old, either. This particular day, the Wasp shaved all of the hair off of her lip and neck and wore a dark blue dress. When she sat across from Mr. Dobbs he barely recognized her, and having no prospects of his own, was immediately transfixed. She bought them fruit wine and cakes, and talked his head off."

"She sounds so nice!" Sylvia was lying on her stomach, her head propped up with her hands.

"Well, you see, Mr. Dobbs was dangerously diabetic. That's why he was so fat and looked so old. Every time he'd mention his insulin, the Wasp would take him by the hand, or kiss him, and the touch of a woman made him forget all about his condition. Eventually, he got in her little red car with her and they drove back to her house— to your house, I suppose.

"Nobody is really sure what happened between Tuesday night and Wednesday afternoon when the police were called—by my dear late husband Charlie—I might add, but it was gruesome. The Wasp waited until he was in a diabetic coma, and then put an IV with sugar water into him."

"What's an IV?" Margot asks.

"Margot, you know what an IV is. Mama uses them on her patients. It's like a needle that puts liquid into you to keep you hydrated," Agatha tells her.

"Yes, Agatha, exactly. Except this IV had sugar water, which is dangerous to anyone, especially someone in a diabetic coma. The police said that Mr. Dobbs only lived a few hours after the Wasp brought him home. Nobody knows why, but his blood was so saturated with sugar that when she dragged him into the backyard, she sliced open his veins and watched hummingbirds drink from him, like a bird feeder. She filleted him. All summer she had built feeders and houses to attract hummingbirds so that when the time came she could watch them drink this man's blood."

Sylvia, Agatha, Teddy, and Margot sat in stunned silence.

"You're making that up!" Teddy protested.

"I am not. Charlie and I were out on the porch when we started to smell something. I was hot and muggy. We didn't think much of it at first, because we so delighted in seeing the hummingbirds bob over the fence. But eventually, Charlie got curious and peaked over the fence. After the trial– she was obviously guilty– the Wasp was locked away in some psychiatric facility– a house for crazy people."

"Why are you telling us this?" Teddy asks. The tea had taken on a musty, metallic luster, and the children all felt they had put too much sugar into theirs.

"I think it's important to know these things. Houses can carry a particular aura. You may want to burn some sage each week. If the spirit of the house makes you ill, now you at least know why. Plus, now you won't be frightened when some bully at school brings it up."

"But we ARE frightened! How could we not be?" Margot protests.

"Well, finish your tea and run along home."

***

It's Margot's first day of high school. She is fourteen and wears her best green corduroy pants and a fuzzy pink sweater. The pants are low rise and the sweater shrugs off of her left shoulder.

"You look ridiculous," Sylvia says, waiting for her siblings to get out of the car. Teddy sighs, kicking open the door of the Grand Am.

"It's cute." Agatha ashes a cigarette out of the window.

"Want me to pick you guys up for lunch?" Sylvia smiles meekly, looking at Margot in the rear view mirror. Margot feels a lump sitting below her sternum. It spreads sharply into her chest, like a shuttlecock. She nods at Sylvia. Agatha and Teddy agree and head towards the school. Sylvia turns to face Margot. "I'll be here 15 minutes before the bell rings, in case you need to get out. I hated this place, but you're a lot smarter than I ever was."

"Am not."

"Are too. Now go. I'll see you in a few hours." Sylvia says. Margot grabs her knapsack from the seat and gets out of the car, "Wait, here." Sylvia rolls the window down and passes two Virginia Slims to Margot. "Ask someone for a lighter. Make friends. The smoking rocks are behind the track."

Sylvia turns up the radio and pulls her sunglasses over her eyes. She watches her sister adjust her posture over and over, walking towards the front doors, trying to find length in her small body, trying to find confidence in the space between her ears and shoulders. Margot wasn't really fat, or chubby even. She just lacked the angles of her siblings, her dark hair and pale skin looked sicklier on her still-round face than on those of the faces of her siblings. Sylvia sighed, thinking about the boys who teased Margot for being from the weird family. Nobody teased her or Teddy or Agatha. Maybe they were too scared. Jamie had told her once that their strange features were 'scary pretty,' but Margot was yet to grow into her pointed chin and constellating freckles. Sylvia missed the sterile halls of the high school the way she missed being stuck in bed after recovering from a long illness. She missed the idleness, the welcome uncertainty. She missed hating high school and growing up.

Sylvia drives out of the parking lot and towards the hay fields, almost gold in the September sun. She shoves a cassette tape into the slot and speeds along the empty back roads. She thinks about calling Jamie. She thinks about hiking into the mountains alone. She thinks about finishing some homework for her correspondence Geology courses. She thinks about the books in her parents' study. All anatomy, human, and animal. Anatomy that her mother guarded with her strong, soft hands, catching babies in pools of water. Anatomy that her father dug out of dead animals with latex gloves on his hands.

Sylvia's mother is tall and striking. Scary-pretty. She keeps her hair shaved close to her skull these days, so that her eyes are the only thing Sylvia can focus on. Lulu's brown eyes are nearly black, and the stubble on her head is black, too. When she stands next to Sylvia's father, she looks like a witch, or an alien, maybe. Casper, in all his pallor, never seems to take his eyes from his wife. His rat-like eyes dance over her strong and lean body, their pinkness like open flesh. Sylvia hates to think of her parents this way, but they are statues, and she admires their hunger for one another, their hunger for the life they built in this strange, small town.

Sylvia picks her siblings up at lunch, after driving down back roads for three hours and singing along to her Nirvana tapes. They eat McDonalds quietly. Margot has chicken nuggets, Agatha a pathetic excuse for a salad, Teddy has the season special: a McLobster. He shovels the sandwich into his mouth with the voracity and crouch of a naked mole rat. Margot picks the batter off of her nuggets before plopping them into her mouth and then sucking plum sauce off her pinky finger. Agatha drinks cup after cup of diet cola. Sylvia's hands shake while she cuts her cheeseburger into tiny squares. She stares into the slick brown of her fourth cup of cheap coffee.

"You know, it's not so bad, guys. My math teacher is really funny and I talked to this really nice boy at the rocks." Margot tells them.

Teddy glares at Sylvia and says "Syl, stop giving Margot cigarettes. She's fourteen."

Ignoring her brother, Sylvia smiles at Margot, "What's his name?"

"Jordan. He says he's Jamie's brother," Margot puts down her burger, "he's kind of cute, too. You know, for a dork."

"Syl definitely thinks his brother's cute. Hey, Syl, if you and Jamie get married, and Jordan and Margot get married, is it incest?" Agatha smirks at Sylvia.

"His brother's just a friend of mine. He's a dork, too."

Every day while Sylvia is enrolled in correspondence Geology classes, she drives her siblings to school, picks them up for lunch, and then drives home again to avoid reading her textbooks. She gives up on the classes before Teddy graduates that year.

***

At fifteen Margot tired of being a member of the "weird" family, and so she bought a red blazer from the Bargain Barn and matching red lipstick from Smith's pharmacy and dropped off the resume she had to make in Life Management class at the local coffee shop. She wore the only black pants she owned, too-small sweatpants that had the rough velour texture of being resold more times than any piece of clothing should be. They sort-of matched the faded black tank top she wore beneath the blazer. She paired the ensemble with an old pair of bright red basketball shoes she found in the shed. Probably Teddy's. She thought the ensemble was really quite splendid. She got the idea for colour blocking from an old edition of Elle magazine her mother left in the basement bathroom.

The interview did not go well. Margot rode her bike home afterwards to cry in the bathtub. She was fifteen and melodramatic, so she sat in her parents' old claw foot tub, fully clothed, and sobbed loudly. She dragged her sister's boom-box into the room, plugged it in and tried to drown out her tears with Britney Spears' "I'm Not a Girl, Not Yet a Woman."

While she was sobbing in the bath, the phone rang. The coffee shop was short-staffed and nobody else had shown up for their interviews. Although she didn't quite have the image they were looking for in a barista, she had the job, if she wanted it.

CHAPTER 15

"Hey, Matt? Want to take Ella to McDonald's today?" Sylvia asks her husband over the last of the coffee Margot gave her, "She's never been and they just renovated the play place."

"Really? You haven't wanted McDonald's for years," Matthew smiles at his wife, putting his book down on the table.

"I've been craving a cheeseburger. I used to take everyone there at lunch when Margot was a freshman. It reminds me of her."

"Of course, Syl. Just let me shower and we can go. We can take Ella to the climbing wall, too, if you like."

Sylvia smiles at her husband as she brushes their daughter's downy hair with a bristled brush. He kisses Ella on the forehead and Sylvia on the cheek before heading to the master bathroom. Sylvia picks up Ella and dances around the room, singing *Heart Shaped Box* slowly to herself, to the tune of a waltz. Margot used to dance with Ella and her own daughters every time she came over for dinner. Ella begins to cry. What was a blissful mother-daughter moment for Sylvia is strange and unfamiliar to Ella. With a sigh, Sylvia pops her daughter into her bouncer and fishes a soother out of the couch cushions. She sucks the lint off before putting it in the wailing child's mouth.

Sylvia turns on the children's radio and begins doing chin ups to the tune of *Twinkle Twinkle Little Star*.

The phone rings. Sylvia ignores it. She wonders why everyone doesn't just text.

"Sylvia, it's Jordan. I'm sorry I couldn't make it to the funeral. I was in Capetown. I just heard. Call me."

"Oh, fuck," Sylvia curses.

Ella spits out the soother. "Oh, fuh!"

"Ella, no! Don't say that. Mommy didn't mean to say that." Matthew re-enters the room in a towel.

"Fuh!"

"Ella, stop it!" Sylvia scolds.

"Who was that on the phone?"

"Jordan."

"Oh, fuck," replies Matthew.

"Fuh!"

The police had tried to contact all of Margot's ex-partners, but with little success. There was a pretty long list of estranged men, and Margot had a habit of burning all their things and blacklisting them from her life. Andrew, her most recent partner, moved to Silicon Valley two years earlier. The father of her second youngest daughter, Geoff, ran off with the Acupuncturist years ago. Nobody knew who the unborn child's father was, and Jordan hadn't called in four years.

Sylvia calls Agatha and Teddy to tell them that she's picking them up to take them to McDonalds. She'll tell them Jordan called over cheeseburgers

***

It is four months after Margot's funeral and Sylvia lies in the bath. She grips the small strip of fat below her navel, digging into it with her nails, and sighs. She falls back into the water, eyes open. She looks at the bathroom lights through the water, blurry halos. Ella fusses in her bouncer just beyond the bath. The water fills Sylvia's ears and quells the sound of the baby. She looks down at her chest. The freckle exactly between her breasts, the black hairs sprouting around her raw nipples, the folds where her breasts recede into her armpits. She holds her breath until she has taken stock of everything she dislikes about herself. She digs her short nails into the divots in her cheeks, the remnants of teenage skin-picking. Her hair is thinning from stress, and when Ella tugs at it, it isn't unusual for a chunk to come out.

Sylvia racks her brain for reasons her sister died. God, maybe, punishing her for having children out of wedlock. Sylvia hated herself for reverting to second-hand Catholic guilt. She remembered the church incense burning in the gymnasium of her catholic school, her atheist parents wanting them to go to the bigger, newer school. If it wasn't God, then why? Chance, maybe, probably. Randomness; oddly specific randomness. Sylvia's mind shifted to Jamie, his advances, her refusal to kiss him when he showed up at her home the week before.

Every time Jamie came up to climb in the Rockies, he and Sylvia grabbed a beer at the hotel. He would tell her about his new tools, his family, and his sexual conquests. He would tell her about his fiancé, how she liked to be tied up. He would tell her about three-somes they had and the other women he slept with on the road. Sylvia would nod amicably and sip at her drink, sometimes indulging in deep fried pickles with tzatziki. Part of her was excited by his feverish talk and strange lifestyle, but more of her feared it. Jamie was toxic, she decided. She had a beautiful baby, a kind and handsome, if a bit doughy, husband, and she was still in shape. Besides, she had done El Cap in a day just after the funeral, so she could climb through the grief, without Jamie.

Ella coos softly. She loves the sound of water sloshing slow in the tub. Sylvia watches the flickering of the candles around the edge of the tub and wonders how parent-teacher interviews are going for Matthew. His students love him. They come back years after they've graduated, take him for drinks, thank him for inspiring them, for guiding them. Every year they receive at least one wedding invitation to a former student's wedding. Sometimes they are high school sweethearts. Sometimes Sylvia goes along to the weddings. She sinks deeper into the tub, warmth spreading all over her body.

She closes her eyes, listening to her daughter's small breaths, and submerges her head, thinking back to Agatha's frantic call the night before.

"A ghost, Aggie? Are you sure? Why were you out running so late?" Sylvia had forgotten about the Bargain Barn. It was where she bought her first climbing gear.

When she opens her eyes the lights are off and Ella has stopped cooing. Sylvia sits up, confused. A dark cloud spreads over her in the tub, in the water where the bubbles have all popped. She jolts, the cloud of black seeping over her, and knocks some candles over with her elbow, some fall into the tub, two fall over the edge onto a pile of towels. Something glass falls to the floor. Something hard brushes against the inside of her thigh. The candles set the towels alight, and Sylvia searches for Ella in the dark, slipping as she gets out of the tub, falling chest first into broken glass and flames. She hears a giggle, a giggle too mature for Ella, and stands up, glass falling. She reaches for the light switch, but instead her hand collides with a small nose. A girl is perched like a monkey on the sink, in front of the switch, the fire from the towels reflected in her dark eyes. Her lopsided bangs and dark freckles bounce as she giggles and leaps at Sylvia.

Sylvia falls backwards, colliding with the toilet, tearing down the shower curtain. Footsteps careen up the stairs.

"Sylvia, babe, what the hell?" Matthew throws open the door, flicking on the light switch. Matthew picks Sylvia up, cradles her in his arms. The black mess in the tub was a glass of red wine, nothing too sinister,

"I grabbed Ella and put her to bed," he tells her, "and then I heard a crash—Jesus Christ, you're bleeding." Matthew carries Sylvia into their bedroom, laying her on white sheets. She is pale, paler than usual. Her long, sinewy body is stretched thin. A gash on her forehead spills blood down her face, over the curves of her cheeks and into her hairline, matting the baby-fine hairs by her ears. Another gash runs down the side of her leg, nearly a foot long, staining the bed sheets. Sylvia stares at the ceiling, mouth ajar.

"Honey, I'm going to get some rubbing alcohol. There's still some glass in your cuts. I need to check on Ella. I'll be right back. You're okay, you're okay." As soon as Matthew is out of the room, running to the first aid kit, Sylvia rolls onto her side, her body convulsing with sobs. The glass digs further into her skin with the pressure of the bed. She pushes her face deep into the pillow and digs her leg into the sheets, the bits of glass burrowing into her skin like maggots into a dead animal.

"Shit, Syl. You're okay," Matthew reenters the room with gauze, tweezers, and alcohol pads, "I think you might need stitches. I'll call Teddy to come get Ella."

"No, no, no," Sylvia mutters, over and over, "I'm okay, I'm just tired."

Matthew turns Sylvia onto her back, maneuvering her tenderly. He kisses her forehead, just left of the gash, and dabs at the wound with a pad. He gingerly plucks out all of the bits of glass, and spreads alcohol in the wound. Sylvia doesn't blink once. Matthew cleans her wounds and wraps her in a thin sheet. He leaves the room and she hears him sweeping the mess in the bathroom. Glass clinks, the vacuum whirs, and then the water comes on.

"Here, love, time to rinse off all of the blood." He picks her up, still wound in the sheet, and places her in the tub. Sylvia wraps her arms around her knees and her husband ladles warm water over her, carefully washing her hair, softly running his hands over her body, rinsing off the blood and wine.

CHAPTER 16

Sylvia and Matthew are in their first couples' counseling appointment when the chief of police calls to tell them that they know who set the fire. Their therapist is a young man, and they are surprised at how much they like him. He asks them to list all of the things that they love about each other, and to tell him what they want their daughter to see in their relationship. Matthew strokes Sylvia's hand, bandages outlining where the glass cut her a week previously. Sylvia tells the therapist that she has always been afraid of being safe, and that Matthew makes her feel so secure that she is terrified of losing herself in the safety. She tells the therapist that since her sister died she is less terrified of safety, but more terrified of being alone. She tells Matthew that she loves him and has always loved him and is only starting to realize that she can love him and Ella and herself at the same time.

***

Agatha and Tasia are eating lunch in the cafeteria of the Foothills hospital when Agatha receives the call that they have found her sister's killer. Agatha wails like a banshee in the cafeteria, pounds her fists against the floor. Tasia covers her with her own body and holds her. They cling to each other in relief and agony. Tasia's supervisor rushes over to see what has happened but the woman cannot speak. Soon after, Agatha resumes work as a midwife full-time, and her and Tasia carpool to work whenever they can, sometimes even working the same shift as nurse and midwife.

***

When Teddy learns that his sister's death is no longer such a mystery, he decides to finish the mobile he was making for Margot's baby. He knows that he should be angry, that he should be looking for a way to confront the man who hurt his sister, but he is so, so tired. He falls asleep at his workbench while stitching together the youngest sister in *Fitcher's Bird*.

***

Mother nature will come for you, in the end. She will consume you. Like Istria before Agatha returned, the bees will use your body as a blueprint for their new home. Mushrooms will sprout from your eye sockets and your flesh and blood will feed beds of wildflowers. Lichen will cling to your bones and small animals will nest in your pelvis. Like Margot, worms will breed in you as decay sets in. Your body will glow and vibrate and sing as mother nature dines on you. She will perform her own kind of taxidermy on your corpse; the kind where you feed the forest instead of the pockets of men. Mother nature will come for you, and everyone you love and everyone you hate. She will reclaim you. All that will remain is a community garden, built on corpses and without the help of people.

Every August, the living Morris siblings get cheeseburgers and sit at the graves of Margot, Lola, Luna, and the baby. Every August, they are greeted by stuffed toys, bouquets of flowers, trinkets, and letters. The Valley might think the Morris family outcasts, freaks, weirdos, etcetera, but the people have not forgotten Margot's smile or the hearts she made in the top of lattes. They have not forgotten how she would give out cookies for free to their children and make homemade dog treats for them to take home. They have not forgotten about the young mother who was killed by someone she trusted. They have not forgotten about the nesting doll funeral, the colony collapse that came after, or the image of Agatha in the snow in the middle of the four-way stop.

Sylvia, Agatha, and Teddy tell Margot about their lives and laugh as they imagine what she would say to them, what her advice might be. Jordan is in jail up near Edmonton but every August they have to throw away a letter addressed to them from him. It is always accompanied by yellow roses, always on the littlest grave. Every August, the siblings talk about the little girl in the red dress that seems to follow them.

THE END

ABOUT THE AUTHOR

Erin Emily Ann Vance is an alumna of the Banff Centre for Arts and Creativity and the Seamus Heaney Centre for Poetry. She holds an MA in English and Creative Writing from the University of Calgary and studies Irish Folklore and Ethnology at University College Dublin. She is the author of three poetry chapbooks, most recently *The Sorceress Who Left too Soon: Poems After Remedios Varo from Coven Editions*. Erin was a recipient of the Alberta Foundation for the Arts Young Artist Prize in 2017, nominated by Aritha van Herk, and was a finalist for the 2018 Alberta Magazine Showcase Awards for fiction for her short story, *All the Pretty Bones,* which appeared in filling station magazine. Her writing has appeared in the Literary Review of Canada, ARC Poetry Magazine, Grain Magazine, Contemporary Verse 2, EVENT Magazine, and more.